" Seized him by the throat "

TIGERS AND TRAITORS

BY

JULES VERNE

AUTHOR OF "TWENTY THOUSAND LEAGUES UNDER THE SEA"
"CLIPPER OF THE CLOUDS," ETC.

Fredonia Books
Amsterdam. Netherlands

Tigers and Traitors

by
Jules Verne

ISBN: 1-58963-448-9

Reprinted from the original edition

Fredonia Books
Amsterdam, The Netherlands
http://www.fredoniabooks.com

In order to make original editions of historical works
available to scholars at an economical price, this
facsimile of the original edition is reproduced from
the best available copy and has been digitally
enhanced to improve legibility, but the text remains
unaltered to retain historical authenticity.

TIGERS AND TRAITORS

———•———

CHAPTER I.

OUR SANATARIUM.

SPEAKING of the great American Andes, the minera-
logist Haüy uses a grand expression when he calls them
" The incommensurable parts of Creation."

These proud words may justly be applied to the
Himalayan chain, whose heights no man can measure
with any mathematical precision.   They occurred to my
mind when I first viewed this incomparable region, in the
midst of which Colonel Munro, Captain Hood, Banks,
and myself were to sojourn for several weeks.

"Not only are these mountains immeasurable," said the
engineer, "but their summits must be regarded as
inaccessible; for human organs cannot work at such
a height, where the air is not dense enough for
breathing!"

This chain may be best described as a barrier of
primitive granite, gneiss, and schist rocks, 1560 miles in
length, extending from the seventy-second meridian to
the ninety-fifth, through two presidencies, Agra and
Calcutta, and two kingdoms, Bhootan and Nepaul.   It
comprehends three distinct zones; the first, 5000 feet
high, being more temperate than the lower plain, and
yielding a harvest of corn in the winter, and rice in the

summer; the second increasing from 5000 to 9000 feet, on which the snow melts in the spring-time ; and the third, rising to 25,000, covered with ice and snow, which even in the hot season defies the solar rays.

At an elevation of 20,000 feet the mountains are pierced by eleven passes, which, incessantly threatened by avalanches, swept by torrents, and encumbered by glaciers, yet make it possible, though dangerous and difficult, to go from India to Thibet. Above this ridge, which is sometimes rounded and then again as flat as Table Mountain at the Cape of Good Hope, rise seven or eight peaks, some volcanic, commanding the sources of the Gogra, the Jumna, and the Ganges. The chief are Mounts Dookia and Kinchinjinga, rising to 21,000 feet; Diodhoonga, 24,000 ; Dhawalagiri, 27,000; Chumalari, 28,000 ; and the highest in the world, Mount Everest, 29,000 feet. Such is this magnificent pile of mountains, which neither Alps, Pyrenees, nor Andes can excel in loftiness, and whose summits not even the most daring of ascensionists have ever ventured to assail.

The first slopes are extensively and thickly wooded. Here may be found different representatives of the palm family, which, in a higher zone, give place to vast forests of oaks, cypress, and pines, to rich masses of bamboos and herbaceous plants.

Banks, who gave us this information, told us also that the snow-line is 12,000 feet lower on the Indian side of the chain than on the Thibetian ; the reason being that the vapours brought by the south winds are arrested by the enormous barrier. On the other side, therefore, villages have been established at an altitude of 15,000 feet in the midst of fields of barley and beautiful meadows. If you believe the natives, one night is sufficient for a crop of grass to carpet these pastures !

In the middle zone, peacocks, partridges, pheasants, bustards, and quails represent the winged tribe. Goats and sheep abound. On the highest zone we only find the wild boar, the chamois, the wild cat, and the eagle soars above the scanty vegetation, mere humble specimens of an arctic flora.

But there was nothing there to tempt Captain Hood. Was it likely that this Nimrod would have come into the Himalayan region merely to continue his trade of domestic provider? Fortunately for him, there was no chance that game worthy of his Enfield rifle and his explosive balls would be scarce.

At the foot of the first slopes of the chain extends a zone, called by the natives the belt of Terrai. It is a long declivitous stretch of land, four or five miles wide, damp, warm, covered with vegetation and dense forests, forming favourite resorts for wild beasts. This Eden of the hunter who loves the stirring features of the chase lay but 1500 yards below us. It was therefore easy to enter into these preserves, which seemed as it were quite distinct grounds.

It was more than probable that Captain Hood would have greater pleasure in visiting the lower than the upper zones of the Himalayas, although, even after the explorations of that most ill-humoured of travellers, Victor Jacquemont, many important geographical discoveries remain yet to be made.

" So this important chain is only very imperfectly known ? " I remarked to Banks.

" Very imperfectly indeed," answered the engineer. " The Himalayan chain may be likened to a little planet stuck on to our globe, and keeping its own secrets."

" They have been surveyed though," said I ; " they have been explored as much as is possible ! "

" Oh, yes ! There has been no lack of Himalayan travellers," replied Banks. "Messrs. Gerard and Webb, the officers Kirkpatrick, Fraser, Hodgson, Herbert, Lloyd, Hooker, Cunningham, Strabing, Skinner, Johnson, Moorcroft, Thomson, Griffith, Vigne, Hügel, the missionaries Huc and Gabet, and more recently the brothers Schlagentweit, Colonel Waugh, Lieutenants Reuillier and Montgomery, have, by dint of great labour,

made known in large measure their orological arrangements.   Nevertheless, my friends, much remains to be
learnt.

"The exact heights of the principal peaks have given
rise to numberless rectifications. Formerly Dhawalagiri was the king of the whole chain ; then after new
measurements, he was forced to yield the throne to
Kinchinjinga, who again has abdicated in favour of
Mount Everest. At the present time, the latter sur-
passes all its rivals.   However, the Chinese now say that
the Kuen-Lun Mountains, to which, it is true, European
measurements have not been applied, surpass Mount
Everest in a slight degree, and that we must no longer
look to the Himalayas as possessing the highest point
of our globe.

"But in reality these measurements must not be considered mathematical until they have been barometically
obtained, and with every precaution that a direct determination will admit of. And how is this to be done
without carrying a barometer to the very top of one of
these inaccessible peaks ? Of course no one has yet
accomplished this."

"It will be done," answered Captain Hood, "just as
some day voyages will be made to both the north and
south pole ! "

"Evidently ! "

"Or an exploring party to the lowest depths of old
Ocean."

"Doubtless."

"Or a journey to the centre of the earth ? "

"Bravo, Hood ! "

"As everything will be done !" I added.

"Even an aerial voyage to each of the planets of the
solar system !" rejoined Hood, whom nothing daunted.

"No, captain," I replied.   "Man, a mere inhabitant of
the earth, cannot overstep its boundaries!   But though
he is confined to its crust, he may penetrate into all its
secrets."

"He can, he must!" cried Banks. "All that is within the limits of possibility may and shall be accomplished. Then when man has nothing more to discover in the globe which he inhabits—"

"He will disappear with the spheroid which has no longer any mysteries concealed from him," put in Captain Hood.

"Not so!" returned Banks. "He will enjoy it as a master, and will derive far greater advantages from it. But, friend Hood, now that we are in the Himalayan country, I wish to tell you of a curious discovery which you may make, amongst others, and which will certainly interest you."

"What is it about, Banks?"

"In the account of his travels, the missionary Huc speaks of a singular tree which is called in Thibet ' the tree of ten thousand pictures.' According to the Hindoo legend, Tong Kabac, the reformer of the Buddhist religion, was changed into a tree some thousand years after the same adventure happened to Philemon, Baucis, and Daphne, those curious vegetable beings of the mythological flora. The hair of Tong Kabac became the foliage of this sacred tree, and on the leaves are—the missionary declares he saw it with his own eyes—Thibetian characters, distinctly to be traced in the veins."

"A tree producing printed leaves!" I exclaimed.

"And, moreover, on which you may read the purest and most moral sentences," continued the engineer.

"That would be well worth the trouble of proving," said I, laughing.

"Prove it, then, my friends," answered Banks. "If these trees exist in the southern part of Thibet, they surely are to be found in the upper zone, on the southern slopes of the Himalayas. During your excursions, then, you can be on the look-out for this—what shall I call it?—this maxim-tree."

"No, by Jove!" returned Captain Hood. "I came

here to hunt, and have not the smallest intention of doing anything in the climbing line."

"Well, my dear fellow," resumed Banks, "a daring climber like you ought to make some ascent in all this great chain."

"Never!" exclaimed the captain.

"Why not?"

"I have renounced ascents!"

"Since when?"

"Since the day when, after having risked my life twenty times," answered Captain Hood, "I managed to reach the summit of Vrige', in the kingdom of Bhootan. It was said that no human being had ever set foot on the top of that peak! There was glory to be gained! my honour was at stake! Well, after no end of narrow squeaks for it, I got to the top, and what did I see but these words cut on a rock: 'Durand, dentist, 14, Rue Caumartin, Paris!' I climb no more!"

The honest captain! I must confess that, while telling us of his discomfiture, Hood looked so comical, that it was impossible to help joining him in a hearty laugh.

I have several times spoken of the "sanatariums" of the peninsula. These resorts in the mountains are much frequented during the summer by landowners, officers, and merchants, who are scorched by the glowing heat of the plains.

In the first rank we must name Simla, situated on the thirty-first parallel, and to the west of the seventy-fifth meridian. It is like a little bit of Switzerland, with its torrents, its streams, its châlets pleasantly situated under the shade of cedars and pines, 6000 feet above the level of the sea.

After Simla, I must mention Darjeeling, with its pretty white houses, overlooked by Mount Kinchinjinga, 312 miles to the north of Calcutta, 6900 feet above the level of the sea, about the eighty-sixth degree of longitude, and the twenty-seventh degree of latitude—a

charming situation, in the most beautiful country in the
world. Other sanatariums there are at different points
of the Himalayan chain.

And now to these fresh and healthy stations, rendered
indispensable by the burning climate of India, was
added our Steam House. But it belonged to ourselves
alone. It offered all the comforts of the most luxurious
dwellings on the peninsula. Here, in this delicious
climate, surrounded by all the necessaries and appli-
ances of modern life, we dwelt in an atmosphere of
quietness which we might have sought for in vain at
Simla or Darjeeling, where there are swarms of Anglo-
Indians.

The site for our sanatarium was judiciously chosen.
The road, leaving the lower part of the mountain, di-
verged at this point both to the east and to the west, so
as to connect several scattered villages. The nearest of
these hamlets was five miles from Steam House. It was
occupied by a hospitable race of mountaineers, who rear
goats and sheep, and cultivate rich fields of wheat and
barley.

Thanks to our able staff of attendants and Banks'
directions, a few hours saw the encampment arranged in
which we were to pass six or seven weeks.

One of the spurs supporting the great framework of
the Himalayas formed a gently undulating plateau,
nearly a mile in length, and half a mile in width. This
was covered with a thick carpet of short, close, velvety
grass, dotted all over with violets. Clusters of beautiful
rhododendrons, as large as small oaks, and natural
arbours of camellias, gave a gay and garden-like aspect
to the scene. Nature had had no need to call in the aid
of workmen from Ispahan or Smyrna, to manufacture
this vegetable carpet. Several million seeds, brought
by the sweet south breezes to the fertile ground, a
little rain, a little sunshine, and there lay the green, soft
fabric!

At least a dozen groups of magnificent trees gave

shade to the plateau. They looked like parties of skirmishers thrown out from the main body—the immense forest which clothed the sides of the spur and the neighbouring heights, eighteen hundred feet above us. Cedars, oaks, the long-leaved pendanus, beech-trees, maples, mingled with bananas, bamboos, magnolias, locust-trees, and Japan fig-trees. Some of these giants reared their lofty heads more than a hundred feet above the soil. They looked quite as if planted on purpose to shelter some woodland dwelling, so the arrival of Steam House was well timed.

The fanciful roofs of the two pagodas matched well with the varied foliage, flowers gay as butterflies, and leaves, some small and delicate, others large and long, and shaped like the paddle of a canoe. The train was quite hidden by all this rich verdure; nothing showed that it was a moving house—it looked fixed to the ground, and as if nothing could induce it to stir.

In the background roared a torrent, whose course could be traced by its silvery gleam many hundred feet, as it descended the mountain-side. It flowed down the right slope of the spur, and plunged, at no great distance from us, into a natural basin, overhung by splendid trees.

The overflow from this basin formed a stream, which, running across our plateau, ended in a noisy cascade, which dashed itself finally into a bottomless gulf.

From this description it may be seen how favourably Steam House was situated, both for comfort for the body and pleasure for the eye. Below us lay other and lesser crests, descending in gigantic steps to the plain. All this we could see from our high place of observation.

Number One of Steam House was placed so that the view to the south might be seen from the verandah as well as from the side windows of the drawing and dining rooms. Over us " a cedar spread his dark-green layers of shade," contrasting with the eternal snow which glittered on the distant mountain peaks.

On the left. Number Two stood close to an enormous granite rock, gilded by the sun. This rock, as much by its strange shape as by its warm colour, reminded us of the gigantic plum-pudding stones, of which M. Russell-Killough speaks in his account of his journey across Southern India.

This, our attendants' house, was placed about twenty feet from the principal dwelling. From the end of one of its roofs curled upwards a little stream of blue-grey smoke, showing the position of Monsieur Parazard's culinary laboratory.

In the midst of the trees which lay between the two habitations might be seen a huge mastodon. It was Behemoth, standing under a great beech-tree, with his trunk upraised, as if browsing on the branches. He, too, was stationary now ; resting, albeit he had no need of rest. However, there he stood, resolute defender of Steam House, like some enormous antediluvian animal, guarding the way.

Colossal as we had always thought our elephant, now that he stood before the everlasting hills, he, the handi-work of puny man, faded into insignificance.

"Like a fly on the façade of a cathedral!" remarked Captain Hood contemptuously.

The comparison was good. Here, behind us, was a block of granite, from which a thousand elephants the size of ours might have been carved, and this block was but a simple step in the stair which leads up and up to the topmost crest crowned by the peak of Dhawalagiri.

At times, when the sky lowers, not only the highest summits, but the lower crests, disappear. This is caused by thick vapours sweeping across the middle zone, and veiling all the upper part. The landscape shrinks, and then, by an optical effect, it is as if the houses, the trees, the rocks, and Behemoth himself, resumed their natural size. When certain moist winds blow, the clouds often roll below the plateau. The eye then rests on nothing but a sea of clouds, illumined here and there by the sun's rays. All land both above and beneath vanishes, and we feel as if transported into some aerial region, beyond the earth.

Suddenly the wind changes. A northern breeze blows through the mountain gulleys, the fog is swept away, the cloudy sea disappears as if by magic, the grand rocks and peaks stand out again, and once more our view extends over a panorama of sixty miles.

CHAPTER II.

MATHIAS VAN GUITT.

AT daybreak on the 26th of June, the jovial tones of a well-known voice aroused me from my slumbers. Captain Hood and his man Fox were engaged in lively conversation in the dining-room, where I soon joined them.

At the same moment Banks made his appearance, upon which the captain greeted him with,—

"Well, Banks, here we are at last, arrived in safety. It's a positive halt this time. Not a mere stoppage for an hour or two, but a stay of some months."

"Very true, my dear Hood," replied the engineer; "now you can arrange your hunting excursions as you please. Behemoth's whistle won't hurry you back to camp."

"Do you hear, Fox?"

"Ay, ay, captain," answered the man.

"St. Hubert be my speed!" cried Hood. "I vow I won't leave this sanatarium, as you call it, until the fiftieth is added to my list! The fiftieth, Fox! I have an idea that that fellow will be particularly hard to get hold of."

"He will be got, though," put in Fox.

"What has put that idea into your head, captain?" I asked.

"Oh, Maucler, it is merely a presentiment—a sportsman's presentiment, nothing more."

"Well, then," said Banks, "from to-day, I suppose, you will leave the encampment, to commence the campaign?"

"From to-day," answered Captain Hood, "we shall

begin by reconnoitring the ground, so as to explore the lower zone, by descending into the Terrai. Provided the tigers have not abandoned their residences."

" Can you imagine such a thing ? "

" Remember ! my bad luck ! "

" Bad luck !—in the Himalayas ! " returned the engineer. " Would that be possible ? "

" Well, we shall see ! You will accompany us, Maucler ? " asked Captain Hood, turning to me.

" Yes, certainly."

" And you, Banks ? "

" I also," replied the engineer ; " and I fancy too that Munro will join you, like myself,—as an amateur."

" Oh," returned Hood, " come as amateurs if you like, but you must be amateurs well armed. It would never do to walk about with nothing but sticks in your hands. The very wild beasts would hide themselves for shame."

" Agreed, then," said the engineer.

" Now, Fox," continued the captain, addressing his servant, " no mistakes this time, please. We are in the tiger country. Four Enfield rifles for the colonel, Mr. Banks, Monsieur Maucler, and myself ; two guns loaded with explosive ball for yourself and Goûmi."

" Don't be afraid, captain," replied Fox. " The game shan't have any reason to complain, I warrant you."

This day was to be devoted to reconnoitring the forest which clothed the lower part of the Himalayas, below our sanatarium.

About eleven o'clock, therefore, Sir Edward Munro, Banks, Hood, Fox, Goûmi, and myself, all well armed, descended the road which slanted towards the plain, taking care to leave behind our two dogs, whose services were not required in an expedition of this sort.

Sergeant McNeil remained in camp with Storr, Kâlouth, and the cook, to complete the arrangements. After his two months' journey, Behemoth required to be examined both inside and out, cleaned, and put in order. This was, of course, a long, minute, and delicate opera-tion, which would give his usual keepers, the driver and stoker, occupation for some time.

Soon after leaving our camp, a turn of the road quite hid Steam House, which disappeared from our sight, behind a thick curtain of trees.

It no longer rained. A fresh wind blew from the north-east, driving the hurrying clouds before it. The sky was overcast, and the temperature consequently suitable for pedestrians, but we missed the pretty variations of light and shade which add such a charm to woodland scenery.

The six thousand feet down a direct road would have been but an affair of five-and-twenty or thirty minutes, but it was lengthened by the windings it took to avoid steep places. It took us not less than an hour and a half to reach the outskirts of the forest, but we all enjoyed the walk.

"Attention!" exclaimed Captain Hood. "We are now entering the domain of tigers, lions, panthers, leopards, and other interesting inhabitants of the Himalayan region. It is very exciting to destroy wild beasts, but it wouldn't be quite so pleasant to be destroyed by them! Therefore, do not stray away from each other, and be prudent."

Such advice from the lips of so bold a hunter was of considerable value, and we respected it accordingly. We all looked to the loading of our guns, and kept our eyes open. I may add that we not only had to be on our guard against wild beasts, but against serpents also, as the most dangerous of their species infest the Indian forests. Belongas, green serpents, whip-snakes are frightfully venomous. The number of victims who succumb annually to the bite of these reptiles is five or six times greater than that of domestic animals or human beings who are killed by wild beasts.

In this region it was no more than the commonest prudence required, to look where you set your foot, or placed your hand, to keep your ears open for the slightest rustle in the grass or bushes, and your eyes, as mush as possible, everywhere at once.

At half-past twelve we were well into the forest. The great trees formed wide alleys through which even Behemoth and his train might have passed with ease. Indeed, this part of the forest had been partially cleared by the hill-men, as we ascertained from the marks their carts had left in the soft clayey ground. The principal alleys ran parallel with the mountain chain, along the greatest length of the Terrai, connecting the glades formed by the woodman's axe, and with more narrow paths which led off from them, and ended in impenetrable thickets.

We followed these avenues, more like surveyors than sportsmen, so as to ascertain their general direction. No roar or scream broke the silence of the wood, but great footprints, plainly recent, showed that wild beasts had not deserted the Terrai.

Suddenly, just as we were turning an angle formed by the hill, an exclamation from Captain Hood brought us all to a standstill.

Twenty paces from us was a construction most peculiar in its shape. It was not a house, for it had neither chimney nor windows.

It was not a hunter's lodge, for it had neither loopholes nor embrasures. It might rather have been taken for a native tomb, lost in the depths of the forest.

Imagine a sort of long cube, formed of trunks placed vertically side by side, fixed firmly in the ground, and connected with the upper part by a thick border of boughs. For a roof, other transverse trunks were strongly mortised into the walls. Evidently the builder of this edifice had determined to make it proof against anything. It was nearly six feet high, and twelve feet by five in length and width. There was no sign of any opening, unless one was hidden by a thick beam, of which the rounded top rose a little above the rest of the building. Above the roof were several long flexible tendrils, curiously arranged and tied together. At the extremity of a horizontal lever, which supported all this, hung a running knot, or rather noose, made of a thick twist of creepers.

" Hallo, what's that ? " I exclaimed.

" That," answered Banks, after examining it well, " is simply a mouse-trap, and I leave you, my friends, to guess what sort of mice it is destined to catch."

" A tiger-trap ? " asked Hood.

" Yes," replied Banks, " a tiger-trap. You see the door is closed by that beam, which was kept up by those tendrils, and which must have dropped when the inner weight was touched by some animal."

" It is the first time," said Hood, " that I ever saw a snare of that kind in an Indian forest. A mouse-trap, indeed ! But it isn't worthy of a sportsman."

" Nor of a tiger," added Fox.

" No doubt," said Banks, " but when it is a question of destroying these ferocious animals, and not merely hunting them for pleasure, the best trap is the one which catches most. Now this appears to me most ingeniously arranged to attract and detain wild creatures, however sly and strong they may be."

" Allow me to remark, my friends," said Colonel Munro, " that since the equilibrium of the weight which holds back the door of the trap has been disturbed, the probability is that some animal is taken in it."

" We shall soon know that," cried Captain Hood, " and if the mouse is not dead—"

The captain, giving force to his words, put his gun at full cock. All followed his example.

We had no doubt now that the erection before us was a trap, which, if it was not the work of a native, at any rate was a very practical engine of destruction, being extremely sensitive and uncommonly strong.

Our arrangements made, Captain Hood, Fox, and Goûmi approached and marched round the snare, examining it minutely.

Not the smallest chink, however, gave them the least glimpse into the interior.

B

They listened attentively. Not a sound betrayed the presence of any living creature. All was silent as the grave.

Hood and his companions came round again to the front. They ascertained that the beam slid up and down in two wide vertical grooves. It was only necessary, therefore, to raise this, and the entrance would be open.

"There's not the slightest sound," said Captain Hood, with his ear close against the door, not even a breath. The mouse-trap is empty !"

"Never mind that, you must be careful," and saying this, Colonel Munro seated himself on the trunk of a fallen tree to the left of the clearing. I placed myself beside him.

"Come, Goûmi," said the captain.

Goûmi, with his supple, well-knit frame, active as a monkey, lithe as a leopard, a regular native acrobat, understood directly what was required of him. His natural adroitness designed him for the service the captain wished done. One spring, and he was on the roof, and grasping one of the rods. Then he crept along the lever till he reached the rope of creepers, and by his weight brought it down to the beam which closed the opening.

The loop was then passed over the head of the beam in a notch made for the purpose. All that now remained to be done was to move it by weighing down the other end of the lever.

The united strength of our little party was required for this, so Colonel Munro, Banks, Fox, and I proceeded to the back of the trap.

Goûmi remained on the roof to look after the lever, in case anything prevented it from working freely.

"I say, you fellows," shouted Captain Hood, "if you want me, I will come ; but if you can do without me, I would prefer to stop where I am, near the opening. If a tiger pops out, he shall be saluted with one shot, at any rate!"

"And will that count for your forty-second?" asked I.

"Why not?" answered Hood. "If I shoot him, he will have fallen in freedom."

"Don't count your chickens before they are hatched," said the engineer.

"Especially when the chicken may turn out to be a tiger," added the colonel.

"Now, my friends," cried Banks, "all together."

The beam was heavy, and did not run easily in the grooves; we managed, however, to move it just a foot from the ground, but then it stuck.

Captain Hood, with his gun at full cock, bent down, expecting to see some huge paw or nose poking out. Nothing was to be seen.

"Once more!" cried Banks.

Goûmi now gave a jerk or two to the lever, and the beam again moved up. Gradually the opening became large enough to give passage even to an animal of great size.

But no creature of any description appeared.

It was possible, after all, that, owing to the noise made around the trap, the prisoner might have retreated into the farthest corner of his prison. He might perhaps be waiting for a favourable opportunity to spring out, overturn anything that opposed him, and disappear in the depths of the forest.

It was very exciting.

At last I saw Captain Hood step forward, his finger on the trigger, and cast a keen glance into the interior of the snare.

The beam was by this time completely raised, and the sunlight streamed freely into the building.

At that moment a slight rustle was heard inside, then a great snore, or rather a tremendous yawn, which had a very suspicious sound.

Evidently an animal was in there, which had been fast asleep and was now awaking.

Captain Hood advanced still nearer, and pointed his gun at a dark object which he now saw moving in a corner. Suddenly a cry of terror burst forth, followed imdiately by these words, spoken in good English,—

"Don't fire! For heaven's sake, don't fire!"

The man who uttered them ran out.

Our astonishment was such that our hands left their grasp of the lever and the beam fell again with a dull sound before the opening.

In the meantime the personage who had so unexpectedly made his appearance came up to Captain Hood, whose gun was aimed full at the stranger's breast, and in a somewhat affected tone, accompanied by an emphatic gesture, "I beg you will lower your weapon, sir," he said. "It is no tiger that you have to deal with."

Captain Hood, after some hesitation, returned his rifle to a less threatening position.

"Whom have I the honour of addressing?" asked Banks, advancing in his turn.

"The naturalist Mathias van Guitt, purveyor of pachydermata, tardigrades, plantigrades, proboscidate animals, carnivora, and other mammalia for the house of Mr. Charles Rice of London, and Messrs. Hagenbeek of Hamburg."

Then indicating us by a comprehensive wave of the arm,—"These gentlemen—?"

"Are Colonel Munro and his travelling companions," answered Banks.

"Taking a walk in the Himalayan forest," resumed the purveyor. "A charming excursion indeed. I am happy to pay my respects to you, gentlemen."

Who could this original be, whom we had met in such a strange way? He looked rather as if his wits had gone astray during his imprisonment in the tiger-trap. Was he mad, or was he in possession of his senses? Lastly, to what order of bimana did this individual belong?

We were about to ascertain all this, and we were destined eventually to learn to know well this singular person, who with perfect truth termed himself a naturalist.

Mathias van Guitt, menagerie purveyor, was a spectacled man of about fifty. His smooth face, his twinkling eyes his turned-up nose, the perpetual stir of his whole person, his exaggerated gestures, suited to each of the sentences which issued from his wide mouth, all combined to make him a perfect type of the old provincial comedian. Who has not, at some time or another, met one of these ancient actors, whose whole existence, limited by a horizon of foot-lamps and drop-scene, has been passed between the green-room and stage of a theatre? Indefatigable talkers, worrying gesticulators, always striking some theatrical attitude or other, and the head, which is too empty at old age to have ever had much in it, carried high in air, and thrown a little back. There was certainly something of the old actor in Mathias van Guitt.

I have heard an amusing anecdote about a poor wretch of a singer, who prided himself on always suiting his actions to the words of his part.

Thus, in the opera of " Masaniello," when he sang,—

"If of a Neapolitan fisher . . ."

his right arm, extended towards the audience, would shake as if he held at the end of a line the fish which had just swallowed his hook. Then continuing,—

" Heaven wish'd to make a monarch,"

whilst one hand was raised towards the roof to indicate Heaven, the other, tracing a circle around his proudly-set head, denoted a royal crown.

" Rebelling against the decrees of destiny,"

his whole body seemed strongly to resist some unseen agency which almost threw him backwards.

" He would say as he steer'd his bark . . . ."

Then his two arms, quickly brought from left to right,

and from right to left, as if moving the scull, showed his skill in guiding a boat.

Well, these gestures, customary with the singer in question, were very similar to those used by Mathias van Guitt. His language was always composed of the choicest terms, and he was sometimes rather annoying to his interlocutors if they could not keep beyond the radius of his gestures.

As we learnt later, from his own mouth, Mathias van Guitt was formerly Professor of Natural History in the Rotterdam Museum, but did not succeed in his teaching. The worthy man was doubtless a subject for much laughter, and though pupils flocked to his chair, it was to amuse themselves, not to learn. In short, circumstances induced him to leave his wearisome, unsuccessful teaching of theoretical zoology, and take to practical zoology in the East Indies. This sort of trade suited him better, and he became the agent of important firms in London and Hamburg, who provide both public and private menageries in the two worlds.

A large order from Europe for wild beasts had now brought him into the Terrai. Indeed, his camp was not more than a couple of miles from the trap out of which we had just extricated him.

But how had the purveyor got into the snare? This Banks soon asked, and the reply was made in high-flown language, adorned with various gestures.

"It was yesterday. Already had the sun completed half his daily round, when the thought occurred to me that I would go and visit one of the tiger-traps erected in the forest. I therefore quitted my kraal, which I trust you will honour with a visit, gentlemen, and soon reached this clearing. My servants were attending to some urgent work, and I did not wish to disturb them. It was imprudent, I confess. When I arrived before this snare, I observed that the moveable beam was raised. From this I drew the logical conclusion that no wild animal had allowed itself to be taken in it. However, wishing to ascertain if the bait was still in its place, and if the working of the weight was in good order, I, with a quick movement, insinuated my body through the narrow aperture."

Here the hand of Mathias van Guitt imitated the graceful undulations of a serpent as it glides through the long grass.

"When I reached the other side of the trap," he continued, "I examined the quarter of a goat, the emanations from which were to attract guests to partake of it from this part of the forest. The bait was intact. I was about to withdraw, when an involuntary blow from my arm displaced the weight, the rope became loose, the beam fell, and I found myself taken in my own snare, without any possible means of escape."

Mathias van Guitt paused a moment to allow us to take in all the gravity of the situation.

"Yet, gentleman," he resumed, "I will not conceal from you that I was first of all struck by the comic view of the matter. I was imprisoned, well! There was no gaoler to open the door of my dungeon, granted! But I thought, indeed, that my people, finding that I did not reappear at the kraal, would become uneasy at my prolonged absence and commence a search which sooner or later would end in my being discovered. It was but an affair of time.

> 'Stone walls do not a prison make,
> Nor iron bars a cage ;
> Minds innocent and quiet take
> That for an hermitage.'

I consoled myself with these thoughts, and the hours passed away without anything occurring to modify my situation. The shades of evening fell, and pangs of hunger made themselves felt. I imagined the best thing I could do would be to cheat time by sleeping. I resigned myself then philosophically, and was soon in the arms of Morpheus. The night was calm, and silence reigned throughout the forest. Nothing troubled my slumber, and perhaps I should even now be oblivious, if it had not been that I was awakened by an unusual noise. The door of the trap rose slowly, the blessed light of day streamed into my darksome retreat, the way of escape was open before me! What was my dismay, when I perceived the instrument of death aimed full at my heart! A moment more and I should have been stretched lifeless on the ground! The hour of my deliverance would have been the last of my life! But the gallant captain soon recognized in me a creature of his own species. And I have still to thank you, gentlemen, for having restored to me my liberty."

Such was our new friend's account of himself. It must be acknowledged that we had some difficulty in keeping our gravity, so absurd were his tone and gestures.

"So, sir," said Banks, "your camp is established in this part of the Terrai?"

"Yes, sir," replied Mathias van Guitt. "As I had the pleasure of informing you, my kraal is not more than two miles from here, and if you will honour it with your presence, I shall be happy to receive you there."

"Certainly, Mr. van Guitt," answered Colonel Munro, "we will come and pay you a visit."

"We are hunters," added Captain Hood, "and the arrangements of a kraal will interest us."

"Hunters!" cried Mathias van Guitt, "hunters!"

And his countenance betrayed that he held the sons of Nimrod in very moderate estimation.

"You hunt wild beasts—for the sake of killing them, doubtless?" he resumed, addressing the captain.

"Only to kill them," replied Hood.

"And I only to catch them," answered the purveyor, with evident pride.

"Well, Mr. van Guitt, we shan't agree upon that point," said Captain Hood.

The purveyor shook his head. The discovery of our hunting propensities was not, however, of importance enough to make him withdraw his invitation. "When you are ready to follow me, gentlemen," said he, bowing gracefully.

But as he spoke, voices were heard in the distance, and very soon half a dozen natives appeared at the other end of the glade.

"Ah! here are my people," said Van Guitt.

Then approaching us closer and placing his finger on his lips,—

"Not a word of my adventure!" he whispered. "The attendants and servants of the kraal must not know that I have been caught in my own trap like some common animal! It would lessen the reputation for wisdom which I endeavour to preserve in their eyes."

Our sign of acquiescence reassured the purveyor.

"Master," said one of the natives, whose impassible and intelligent countenance attracted my attention; "master, we have been searching for you for more than an hour, without—"

"I was with these gentlemen, who wish to accompany me to the kraal," answered Van Guitt. "But before quitting the clearing, the trap must be put in order."

Whilst the natives were proceeding to obey their master's orders, Mathias van Guitt invited us to visit the interior of the trap.

Captain Hood entered with alacrity, and I followed.

The space was somewhat limited for the display of our host's gestures, but he nevertheless did the honours as though it were a drawing-room.

"I congratulate you," said Hood, after examining the apparatus. "It is exceedingly well contrived."

"I do not hesitate to say that it is, captain," replied Van Guitt. "This description of snare is infinitely preferable to the ditches set with stakes of hardened wood, or the flexible branches of trees bent together so as to form a running knot. In the first case, the animal is impaled on the sharp points; in the second, it is strangled. That, of course, matters little when the object is merely to kill and destroy. But I, who now speak to you, must procure the living creature intact, with not the slightest blemish."

"Certainly," said Captain Hood; "we do not proceed in the same way."

"Mine is perhaps the best," said the purveyor. "If you were to consult the animals themselves—"

"But I have no intention of consulting them," replied the captain.

Mathias van Guitt and Captain Hood would have some trouble in getting on together, most decidedly.

"Now when the animals are caught in the trap," I asked, "what do you do next?"

"A rolling cage is bought close to the trap," replied Van Guitt, "the prisoners run into it of their own accord, and then all I have to do is to convey them to the kraal, drawn at a slow and steady pace by my domestic buffaloes."

Scarcely were these words uttered when cries arose outside. Captain Hood and I immediately hastened out of the building.

What had happened?

A whip-snake, of the most venomous species, lay on the ground, cut in two pieces by a rod which one of the natives held in his hand, just as it was darting at the colonel.

The man was the one I had at first remarked, and his rapid intervention had certainly saved Sir Edward from immediate death, as we soon saw.

The cry we had heard was uttered by another of the servants, who now lay on the grass in the agonies of death. By a deplorable fatality, the head of the snake, as it was severed from the body, had bounded against the unfortunate man's chest, its fangs had entered him, and, penetrated by the subtle poison, in less than a minute he was dead, all help proving unavailing.

Rousing ourselves from the horror caused by this dreadful sight, we ran up to Colonel Munro.

"You are not hurt?" exclaimed Banks, grasping his hand.

"No, Banks, no, make yourself easy," answered Sir Edward.

Then advancing towards the native, to whom he owed his life, "I thank you, friend," he said.

The native made a sign as if to say that no thanks were necessary, for that.

"What is your name?" asked the colonel.

"Kâlagani," answered the Hindoo.

CHAPTER III.

THE KRAAL.

THE death of this unfortunate man made a deep impression upon us, both from the fact itself and from the cause, though it was anything but an unusual occurrence. It was but one more added to the thousands who annually fall victims in India to the formidable reptiles.[1]

It has been said,—jestingly, I presume,—that formerly there were no snakes in Martinique, but that the English imported them when they were obliged to give up the island to France. The French had no occasion to retaliate in this manner when they yielded their conquests in India, for nature had shown herself only too prodigal in that respect.

Under the influence of the venom, the body of the Hindoo began to exhibit signs of rapid decomposition. A speedy burial was necessary. His companions, therefore, set to work, and soon laid him in a grave deep enough to protect the body from wild beasts.

When this sad ceremony was ended, Mathias van Guitt invited us to accompany him to his kraal, and we readily did so.

Half an hour's walk brought us to the place, which deserved its name of " kraal," though it is a word more especially used by the settlers of South Africa.

It was a wide enclosure, standing in a glade in the depths of the forest. Mathias van Guitt had arranged it with a perfect understanding of the requirements of his trade. A row of high palisades, having a gate wide

---

[1] In 1877, 1677 human beings perished from snake-bites. The rewards paid by Government for the destruction of these reptiles show that in the same year 127,295 were killed.

enough to admit carts, surrounded it on the four sides. Inside was a long hut, made of trunks of trees and planks, which was the dwelling-place.

Six cages, divided into several compartments, and each mounted on four wheels, were drawn up in the left end of the enclosure. From the roars which issued from them, we concluded they were not untenanted.

To the left were penned a dozen buffaloes, which were fed on the mountain grass. These were the animals used to draw the travelling menagerie. Six men, who attended to these creatures and drove the carts, and ten others who were especially skilful in the chase, completed the staff of attendants in the kraal.

The carters were hired only for the duration of the campaign. Their services ended by driving the carts to the nearest railway-station. There the cages were placed on trucks, and wheeled off, *viâ* Allahabad, to Bombay or Calcutta.

The hunters, who were Hindoos, are called " shikarries." They were employed to discover and follow up the traces of animals, dislodge them, and then assist in their capture.

Mathias van Guitt and his men had lived for some months in this kraal. They were there exposed, not only to the attacks of ferocious beasts, but also to the fevers with which the Terrai is infested. The damp nights, the pernicious evaporations from the ground, the moist heat hanging about under the thick-growing trees, through which the sun never penetrates, all combine to make this lower zone of the Himalayas a most unhealthy region.

The purveyor and his men were, however, so well acclimatized, that the malaria affected them no more than it did the tigers or other inhabitants of the Terrai.

It would not have been wise for us to live in the kraal, nor did this enter into Captain Hood's plan. Except for a night or two passed on the watch, we intended living in Steam House, which was too high up for any baleful vapours to reach us there.

Here were we, then, arrived at Van Guitt's encamp. ment. The door opened for us to enter.

Mathias van Guitt appeared particularly flattered by our visit.

" Now, gentlemen," he said, "permit me to do the honours of my kraal. This establishment is replete with every necessary for the pursuit of my vocation. In reality, it is but a hut on a large scale, which, in this country, hunters call a ' houddi.' "

Saying this, our host opened the door of the dwelling which he and his people occupied together. Nothing could have been more simple. One room for the master, another for the carters, and another for the shikarries. A fourth, rather larger, serving for both kitchen and dining-room.

After visiting the habitation of " these bimana, belonging to the highest order of mammalia," we were requested to look at the nearest of the quadrupeds' dwellings.

This was the most interesting part of the kraal. The cages were not like the comfortable dens of a zoological garden, but recalled rather the appearance of a travelling show. All that was required to complete them was a gaudily-painted canvas hung above a stage, and representing in startling colours a tamer, in pink tights and velvet jacket, striking an attitude in the midst of a bounding herd of wild beasts, who, with bloody jaws and claws outspread, were cowering under the lash of some heroic Van Amburgh.

But such a picture would have been wasted on the desert air, as the public were not there to see and be edified by it.

A few paces further on were the buffaloes. They occupied a portion of the kraal on the right, and their daily rations of fresh grass were brought to them there. It would have been impossible to allow these animals to stray in the neighbouring pastures. As Mathias van

Guitt elegantly remarked, "The freedom of pasture, allowable in the United Kingdom, is incompatible with the dangers presented by the Himalayan forests."

The menagerie, properly so called, comprised six cages on wheels. Each cage, with a barred front, was divided into three compartments. Doors, or rather partitions, moved from the top, made it easy for the animals in one compartment to be driven into another, when necessary.

The cages at the present time contained seven tigers, two lions, three panthers, and a couple of leopards.

Van Guitt informed us that his stock would not be complete until he had captured two leopards, three tigers, and one lion more. Then he intended leaving this camp, proceeding to the nearest railway-station, and thence travelling to Bombay.

The wild beasts were easily watched in their cages, and proved to be magnificent creatures, but particularly ferocious. They had been too recently caught to have yet become accustomed to a state of captivity. This was plain from their constant roars, their restless pacings up and down, and the blows they gave the bars, straining them in many places.

On seeing us, their rage was redoubled; but Van Guitt was not in the least disturbed.

"Poor beasts!" remarked Captain Hood.

"Poor beasts!" echoed Fox.

"Do you believe, then, that they are more to be pitied than those which you kill?" asked our host, somewhat sharply.

"Less to be pitied than blamed . . . for allowing themselves to be caught!" returned Hood.

If it is true that the wild beasts of a country such as Africa are sometimes compelled to undergo a long fast, because the animals upon which they feed are scarce, such could never be the case in the Terrai zone. Here abound bisons, buffaloes, zebras, boars, antelopes, to which the lions, tigers, and panthers are constantly giving chase. Besides goats and flocks of sheep, not to mention the poor ryots who are their shepherds, offer a certain and easy prey. They always find abundance in the Himalayan forests to satisfy their hunger.

The purveyor fed his menagerie chiefly on the flesh of bison and zebras, and it was the shikarries' duty to procure this meat.

It is a mistake to imagine that this species of hunting is without danger. Quite the contrary. The tiger himself has much to fear from the savage buffalo, who is a terrible animal when wounded. Many a hunter has, to his horror found his antagonist rooting up, with its horns, the tree in which he has taken refuge.

It is said that the eye of a ruminant is a regular magnifying lens, increasing the size of an object three-fold, and that man, in this gigantic aspect, awes him. It is also asserted that the upright position of a human being walking is of a nature to terrify ferocious animals, and, therefore, that it is far better to face them standing than lying or crouching down.

I cannot tell how much truth there may be in these statements ; but it is very certain that a man, even when drawn up to his full height, produces no effect whatever on the savage buffalo; and if his shot misses, he is almost certainly lost.

The buffalo of India has a short, square head, smooth horns, flattened at the base, a humped back—like its American congener—its legs, from the foot to the knee, being white, and its size, from the root of the tail to the end of its muzzle, measuring sometimes twelve feet. Although it is not particularly ferocious when feeding in herds on the plain, it yet is very formidable to any hunter who rashly attacks it.

Such were the ruminants destined to feed the beasts in Van Guitt's menagerie. That they might obtain them with greater certainty and less danger, the shikarries preferred to trap them.

The purveyor, who knew his business, was very sparing as to his captives' food. Once a day, at twelve o'clock,

four or five pounds of meat were given them, and nothing
more. He even, though not from any religious motive,
allowed them to fast from Saturday to Monday. They
must have passed a dismal Sunday! Then, when forty-
eight hours had elapsed, and their modest pittance
appeared, the excitement and the roaring may be
imagined, the cages actually swaying backward and
forwards with the movement of the springing, bounding
creatures inside.

Yes, poor beasts! we may be tempted to say with
Captain Hood. But Mathias van Guitt did not act thus
without a motive; and this enforced abstinence was good
for the animals, and heightened their price in the
European market.

It may easily be imagined that while Van Guitt was
exhibiting his collection, more as a naturalist than a
showman, his tongue was not allowed to stand still. On
the contrary. He talked, he described, he related; and
as wild beasts were the principal subjects of his
redundant periods, it was all tolerably interesting to
us.

"But, Mr. van Guitt," said Banks, "can you tell me if
the profits of the trade are in proportion to the risks that
are run?"

"Sir," answered the purveyor, "it was formerly extremely remunerative. However, for the last few years,
I have been forced to perceive that ferocious animals
have declined. You may judge of this by the current
prices of the last quotation. Our principal market is the
Zoological Garden in Antwerp. Volatiles, ophidians,
specimens of the simian and saurian family, representatives
of the carnivora of both hemispheres, such is the
consuetudinal . . ."

At this word Captain Hood bowed.

". . . produce of our adventurous battues in the forests
of the peninsula. From one cause or another the public
taste seems to have altered, and the sale price is
sometimes less than what was expended on the capture!

c

For instance, a male ostrich is now sold but for 44*l.*, and the female for 32*l.* A black panther found a purchaser for only 60*l.*, a Java tigress for 96*l.*, and a family of lions —father, mother, uncle, and two healthy cubs—were sold in a lump for 280*l.*"

"They really went for nothing," said Banks.

"As to proboscidate animals . . ." resumed Van Guitt.

"Proboscidate?" said Captain Hood.

"We call by that scientific name those pachydermata which nature has furnished with a trunk."

"Such as elephants!"

"Yes, elephants since the quaternary period. They were 'mastodons' in the pre-historic times."

"Thank you," replied Hood.

"As to proboscidate animals," resumed Van Guitt, "we must soon renounce even their capture, unless it is for the sake of their tusks ; for the consumption of ivory has in no way diminished. But since the authors of dramatic pieces, at their wits' end for some novelty, have conceived the idea of introducing these creatures on the stage, they are taken about from one town to another ; so that the same elephant, parading the country with a strolling company, satisfies the curiosity of a whole province. From this cause, elephants are in less request than formerly."

"But," I asked, "do you only supply European menageries with these specimens of the Indian fauna?"

"You will pardon me," replied Mathias van Guitt, "if on this subject, sir, I allow myself, without being too curious, to put to you a simple question?"

I bowed in token of acquiescence.

"You are French, sir," said the purveyor. "That is plainly seen, not only by your accent, but by your type, which is an agreeable combination of the Gallo-Roman and the Celt. Now, as a Frenchman, you cannot have any propensity for distant journeys, and probably have not made the tour of the world?"

Here Van Guitt's hand described one of the great circles of the sphere.

"I have not yet had that pleasure," I replied.

"I will ask you, then, sir," continued our friend, "not if you have been to the Indies, as you are already here, but if you are thoroughly acquainted with the Indian peninsula?"

"Imperfectly as yet," I answered. "However, I have already visited Bombay, Calcutta, Benares, Allahabad, and the valley of the Ganges. I have seen their monuments, I have admired—"

"Ah! what is that, sir, what is all that?" interrupted Mathias van Guitt, turning away his head, and shaking his hand, in a manner to express supreme disdain.

Then launching out into an animated description,—

"Yes, what is all that, if you have not visited the menageries of those powerful rajahs, who maintain the worship of the superb animals, on which the sacred territory of India prides itself? Resume your tourist's staff, sir. Go into Guicowar, and render homage to the King of Baroda. Inspect his menageries, which owe the greater number of their tenants, lions from Kattiwar, bears, panthers, cheetahs, lynx, and tigers, to me. Be present at the celebration of the marriage of his sixty thousand pigeons, which takes place every year, with great pomp! Admire his five hundred bulbuls, the nightingales of the peninsula, whose education is attended to as carefully as if they were heirs to the throne! Contemplate the elephants; one of them is the executioner, and his business it is to dash the head of the condemned man on the stone of punishment! Then transfer yourself to the establishments of the Rajah of Maissour, the richest of Asiatic sovereigns. Enter his palace, where you may count hundreds of rhinoceri, elephants, tigers, and every creature of high rank which belongs to the animal aristocracy of India! And when you have seen all this, sir, perhaps you need no longer be accused of ignorance of the marvels of this incomparable country!"

I could do no more than bow before these remarks. Van Guitt's impassioned style of representing things admitted of no discussion.

Captain Hood, however, pressed him more directly about the particular fauna of this region of the Terrai.

"A little information, if you please," he said, "about the wild beasts which I have come to this part of India to hunt. Although I am only a sportsman, and I repeat, I do not compete with you, Mr. van Guitt, yet if I could be of any use in capturing the tigers which you still want for your collection, I shall only be too pleased to do so. But, when your menagery is completed, you must not take it ill if I, in my turn, shoot a few for my own personal amusement."

Mathias van Guitt put himself into the attitude of a man who has resigned himself to submit to what he disapproves of, but does not know how to prevent. He admitted, however, that the Terrai contains a considerable number of troublesome animals, in no great request in the European markets, so that their sacrifice might be permitted.

"Kill the boars, I consent to that," said he. "Although these swine of the order of pachydermata, are not carnivorous—"

"Carnivorous?" said Captain Hood.

"I mean by that, that they are herbivorous; their ferocity is so great, that hunters who are rash enough to attack them run the greatest danger."

"And wolves?"

"Wolves are numerous all over the peninsula, and are much to be dreaded when they advance in herds on some solitary farm. These animals slightly resemble the wolf of Poland, and I certainly have not much esteem either for jackals or wild dogs. I do not deny the ravages they commit, and as they have not the smallest marketable value, and are unworthy to figure amongst the higher classes of zoo-ocracy, 1 will abandon them also to you, Captain Hood."

" And bears ? " I next asked.

" Bears are good, sir," answered the zoologist with a nod of approval. "Although those of India are not sought for quite as eagerly as others of the family Ursidæ, they nevertheless possess a certain commercial value which recommends them to the benevolent attention of connoisseurs. Your taste might hesitate between the two species which we find in the valleys of Cashmere and the hills of Rajmahal. But, except perhaps in the hibernating period, these creatures are almost inoffensive, and, in short, would not tempt the cynegetic instincts of a true sportsman, such as I hold Captain Hood to be."

The captain smiled in a significant manner, showing well that with or without the permission of Mathias van Guitt, he meant only to refer to himself on these special questions.

" These animals," continued Van Guitt, "feed only on vegetables, and have nothing in common with the ferocious species, on which the peninsula so justly plumes itself."

" Do you include the leopard in your list of wild beasts ? " asked Captain Hood.

" Most certainly, sir. This creature is active, bold, full of courage, and he can climb trees, so for that reason he is sometimes more formidable than the tiger."

" Oh ! " ejaculated the captain.

" Sir," answered Mathias van Guitt in a dignified tone, " when a hunter is no longer sure of finding a refuge in trees, he is very near being hunted in his turn ! "

" And the panther ? " asked Captain Hood, willing to cut short this discussion.

" The panther is superb," answered Mathias van Guitt ; " and you may observe, gentlemen, that I have some magnificent specimens. Astonishing animals, which by a singular contradiction, an antilogy, to use an uncommon word, may be trained for the chase. Yes, gentlemen, in Guicowar especially, the rajahs use panthers in this noble exercise. They are taken out in a palanquin, with their head muffled like a falcon or a merlin! Indeed, they are regular four-footed hawks! No sooner do the hunters come in sight of a herd of antelopes, than the panther is unhooded, and flies upon the timid ruminants, whose feet, swift as they are, cannot carry them beyond the reach of those terrible claws! Yes, captain, yes! You will find panthers in the Terrai! You may perhaps find more than you care for, but I warn you charitably that they are by no means tame!"

"I should hope not," was Captain Hood's reply.

"Nor the lions either," added the zoologist, somewhat vexed at this answer.

"Ah! lions!" said Hood. "Let us speak a little about lions, please!"

"Well, sir," resumed Mathias van Guitt, "I regard the so-called king of beasts as inferior to his congeners of ancient Libya. Here the males do not wear that mane which is the appendage of the African lion, and in my opinion, they are, therefore, but shorn Sampsons! They have, besides, almost entirely disappeared from Central India to seek a refuge in the Kattiwar peninsula, the desert of Theil, and the Terrai forest. These degenerate felines, living solitary, like hermits, do not gain strength by frequenting the company of their fellows. Therefore, I do not give them the first place in the scale of quadrupeds. Indeed, gentlemen, you may escape from a lion, from a tiger, never!"

"Ah! tigers!" cried Captain Hood.

"Yes, tigers!" echoed Fox.

"The tiger," replied Van Guitt, growing animated, "to him belongs the crown. We speak of the royal tiger, not the royal lion, and that is but justice. India belongs entirely to him, and may be summed up in him. Was he not the first occupant of the soil? Was it not

his right to look upon as invaders, not only the representatives of the Anglo-Saxon race, but also the polar
race? Is he not indeed the true child of this sacred
land of Aryvarta? These magnificent animals are
spread over the whole surface of the peninsula, and they
have not abandoned a single district of their ancestors,
from Cape Comerin to the Himalayan barrier!"

And Mathias van Guitt's arm, stretched out to denote
the southern promontory, was now waved northwards
towards the mountain peaks.

"In the Sunderbunds," he continued, "they are at
home! There they reign as masters, and woe to all
who attempt to dispute with them their territory! In
the Neilgherry Hills they roam about in a body, like
wild cats.

'Si parva licet componere magnis!'

You can understand from this why these superb felidæ
are in such demand in all European markets, and are
the pride of menageries! What is the great attraction
in the public or private wild beast show? The tiger!
When do you most fear for the life of the tamer?
When he is in the tiger's cage! For what animals do
the rajahs pay their weight in gold to obtain them to
ornament their royal gardens? The tiger! What
creature is always at a premium in the wild animal
market exchange of London, Antwerp, and Hamburg?
The tiger! In what chase do British officers in India so
distinguish themselves? In the tiger hunt! Do you
know, gentlemen, what entertainment the independent
sovereigns of India provide for their guests? A royal
tiger in a cage is brought. The cage is placed in the
midst of a wide plain. The Rajah, his guests, his officers,
his guards, are armed with lances, revolvers, and rifles,
and are, for the most part, mounted on gallant
solipeds—"

"Solipeds?" said Captain Hood.

"Their horses, if you prefer the more vulgar word.
Already the solipeds, terrified by the near neighbour-

hood of the tiger, his scent, and the light which gleams from his eyes, rear, so that it requires all their rider's skill to manage them. Suddenly the door of the cage is thrown open. The monster springs forth; with wild leaps he flies on the scattered groups; in his fury he immolates a hecatomb of victims. Although sometimes he contrives to break through the circle of fire and sword with which he is surrounded, more often he is overcome and falls, one against a hundred. But, at least, his death is a glorious one, it is avenged beforehand."

"Bravo, Mr. van Guitt," cried Captain Hood, in his turn becoming quite excited. "Yes, that must be a fine sight. Truly the tiger is the king of beasts."

"A royalty too, which defies revolutions," added the zoologist.

"You have caught many, Mr. van Guitt," said Hood, "I have killed many, and I hope not to leave the Terrai until the fiftieth has fallen by my shot."

"Captain," said the purveyor with a frown, "I have delivered up to you boars, wolves, bears, and buffaloes, will not those suffice to gratify your sporting mania?"

I saw that our friend Hood would burst forth with as much animation as Mathias van Guitt on this exciting question. Had the one captured more tigers than the other had killed? Was it better to catch or shoot them? This was the matter and theme of discussion!

Thereupon the captain and the zoologist commenced to exchange rapid sentences, both speaking at once, and apparently not in the least comprehending what the other said.

Banks interposed.

"That tigers are the kings of creation is understood, gentlemen, but I must be permitted to add that they are very dangerous to their subjects. In 1862, if I am not mistaken, these excellent felidæ devoured all the telegraph clerks in the Island of Sangor. We are also told of a tigress who, in three years, made no less than a hundred and eighteen victims, and another, who in the same space of time destroyed a hundred and twenty-seven persons. That is rather too much, even for a queen. Lastly, since the mutiny, in an interval of three years, twelve thousand five hundred and fifty-four individuals have perished by tigers' teeth or claws."

" But, sir," replied Van Guitt, "you seem to forget that these animals are omophagæ."

" Omophagæ ? " said Captain Hood.

" Yes, eaters of raw flesh, and the natives say that when they have once tasted human flesh, they never care for any other ! "

"Well, sir ? " said Banks.

"Well, sir," answered Mathias van Guitt, smiling, "they obey their nature ! . . . They certainly must eat ! '

CHAPTER IV.

A QUEEN OF THE TERRAI.

THIS remark of the zoologist ended our visit to the kraal, as it was time to return to Steam House.

I must say that Captain Hood and Mathias van Guitt did not part the best friends in the world. One wished to destroy the wild beasts of the Terrai, the other wished to catch them ; yet there were plenty to satisfy both.

It was, however, agreed that intercourse between the kraal and the sanitarium should be frequent. Each was to give information to the other. Van Guitt's shikarries, who were well acquainted with this sort of expedition, and knew every turn of the forest, were to render a service to Captain Hood by showing him the tracks of animals. The zoologist most obligingly placed all his men, and especially Kâlagani, at his disposal. This native, although but recently engaged at the kraal, showed himself very intelligent, and completely to be depended on.

In return, Captain Hood promised, as far as lay in his power, to aid in the capture of the animals which were yet wanting to complete the stock of Mathias van Guitt.

Before leaving the kraal, Sir Edward Munro, who probably did not purpose making many visits there, again thanked Kâlagani, whose intervention had saved him. He told him that he should always be welcome at Steam House.

The native saluted coldly. Although he must have felt some sentiment of satisfaction at hearing the man

whose life he had preserved speak thus, he allowed no
tiace of it to appear on his countenance.

We returned in time for dinner. As may be imagined,
Mathias van Guitt was our chief subject of conversation.

"By Jove! what an absurd fellow he is," said the captain. "What with his gestures, his fine choice of words,
and his grand expressions, he is a caution! Only, if he
fancies that wild beasts are mere subjects for exhibition,
he is greatly mistaken!"

On the three following days, the 27th, 28th, and 29th
of June, rain fell with such violence, that our hunters,
to their great annoyance, could not dream of leaving
Steam House. In such dreadful weather it would be
impossible to find a track, and the carnivora, who are no
fonder of water than are cats, would not willingly leave
their dens.

At last the weather showed signs of clearing, and
Hood, Fox, Goûmi, and I made preparations for
descending to the kraal.

During the morning, some mountaineers came to pay
us a visit. They had heard that a miraculous pagoda
had been transported to the Himalayas, and a lively
feeling of curiosity had in consequence brought them to
Steam House.

They were fine types of the Thibetian frontier race.
Full of warlike virtues, of tried loyalty, practising liberal
hospitality, and far superior, both morally and physically, to the natives of the plains.

The supposed pagoda astonished them; but Behemoth
so impressed them as to draw from them marks of
adoration. He was now at rest, what would not these
good people have felt if they had seen him, vomiting
forth flame and smoke, and ascending with a steady step
the rough slopes of their mountains!

Colonel Munro gave a kind reception to these men,
who usually frequented the territories of Nepaul, on the
Indo-Chinese boundary. The conversation turned for a

time on that part of the frontier where Nana Sahib had
taken refuge, after the defeat of the sepoys.

These hillmen knew scarcely so much as we did ourselves on this matter. The rumours of the nabob's
death had reached them, and they cast no doubt upon
it. As to those of his companions who had survived,
perhaps they had sought a more secure refuge in the
depths of Thibet; but to find them in that country
would have been difficult.

Indeed, if Colonel Munro, in coming to the north of
the peninsula, had had any idea of throwing light on
Nana Sahib's history, this reply should have satisfied him.
In listening to our visitors he remained thoughtful, and
took no more part in the conversation.

Captain Hood put some questions to them, but on
quite another point. He learnt that wild beasts, more
particularly tigers, had made frightful ravages in the
lower zone of the Himalayas. Farms, and even whole
villages, had been deserted by their inhabitants. Many
flocks of goats and sheep had been already destroyed,
besides numerous victims among the natives. Notwithstanding the considerable sum offered by the government—three hundred rupees for every tiger's head—the
number of these creatures did not appear to diminish,
and people were asking themselves whether they would
not soon be obliged to leave the country to them
entirely.

The hillmen also added this information, that the
tigers did not confine themselves entirely to the Terrai.
Whenever the plain offered them tall grass, jungle, and
trees among which they could crouch, there they might
be met with in great numbers.

" The evil beasts ! " was their expression.

These honest people had very good cause not to
profess the same opinions on the subject of tigers as the
zoologist Mathias van Guitt and our friend Captain
Hood.

The mountaineers retired, enchanted with the reception they had met with, and promising to repeat their visit to Steam House.

After their departure our preparations were completed, and Captain Hood, our two companions, and I, all well armed ready for any encounter, descended to the Terrai.

On arriving at the clearing, in which was the trap from which we had so fortunately extracted Mathias van Guitt, that gentleman presented himself before our eyes, not without some ceremony.

Five or six of his people, Kâlagani among the number, were occupied in getting a tiger which had been caught during the night, from the snare into a travelling-cage.

It was a magnificent animal indeed, and, as a matter of course, caused Captain Hood to feel corresponding envy.

"One less in the Terrai!" he murmured, between two sighs which found their echo in Fox's manly breast.

"One more in the menagerie," replied the zoologist. "Still two tigers, a lion, and two leopards, and I shall be in a position to honour my engagements before the end of the season. Will you come with me to the kraal, gentlemen?"

"Thank you," said Captain Hood; "to-day, however, we are out on our own account."

"Kâlagani is at your disposal, Captain Hood," replied the purveyor. "He is well acquainted with the forest, and may be useful to you."

"We will gladly take him as a guide."

"Farewell, gentlemen," said Van Guitt; "I wish you good sport! But promise me not to massacre them all."

"We will leave you a few," returned Hood.

And Mathias van Guitt, saluting us with a superb bow, followed his cage, and soon disappeared among the trees.

"Forward!" said Hood, "forward, my men. Hurrah for my forty-second!"

"And my thirty-eighth!" responded Fox.

"And my first!" I added.

But the quiet way in which I uttered the words, made the captain laugh. Evidently, I did not feel the sacred fire.

Hood turned to Kâlagani.

"So you know the forest well?" he asked.

"I have been over it twenty times, day and night, in every direction," replied the man.

"Have you heard that a particular tiger has been lately noticed near the kraal?"

"Yes; but this tiger is a tigress. She has been seen two miles from here, in the upper part of the forest, and they have been trying to get hold of her for several days. Should you like—"

"That's just what we want!" answered Captain Hood, without giving the native time to finish his sentence.

To follow Kâlagani was the best thing we could do, so we did it.

Wild beasts were apparently very plentiful in the Terrai, but here, as everywhere else, each required two bullocks a week for their own particular consumption! Just calculate what the cost of such a "keep" would be to the entire peninsula.

It must not be imagined that the numerous tigers visit inhabited country unless impelled by necessity. Till urged by hunger, they remain hidden in their lairs, and it would be a mistake to imagine that they are met with at every step. Very many travellers have journeyed through these forests without even catching a glimpse of one. When a hunt is organized, the first thing to be done is to reconnoitre the places most frequented by the animal, and especially to find out the stream or spring to which he comes to slake his thirst.

Sometimes this is not sufficient, and he has to be attracted to the spot. This is done easily enough by putting a quarter of beef tied to a stake in some place surrounded by trees and rocks to shelter the hunters. This, at least, is the way they proceed in the forest.

In the plains, it is another thing, and there the elephant becomes the most useful auxiliary to man in his dangerous sport. These animals have, however, to be trained to the work, though even then, they are sometimes seized with a panic which renders the position of the men perched on their backs, dangerous in the extreme. It must also be said that sometimes the tiger does not hesitate to spring on the elephant. The struggle between the man and beast then takes place on the very back of the gigantic steed, and it is rarely indeed that it does not end in favour of the tiger.

In this way the grand hunts of the rajahs and great sportsmen of India are conducted, but it was by no means Captain Hood's manner of proceeding. He was going to search for tigers on foot, and it was on foot that he was accustomed to fight them.

In the meantime, we were following Kâlagani, who was walking on at a round pace. Reserved as all Hindoos are, he spoke little, and contented himself with replying briefly to the questions which we put to him.

After walking for an hour, we halted by a rapid stream, and on its banks were the still fresh tracks of animals. In a little glade was a stake, to which was fastened a quarter of beef. The bait had not been entirely untouched. It had been recently gnawed by the teeth of jackals, those thieves of the Indian fauna, always in quest of prey, but this was not intended for them. A dozen or so of these creatures fled at our approach, and left the place clear.

"Captain," said Kâlagani, "we must wait for the tigress here. You see that it is a good place for an ambush."

It was, indeed, easy to post ourselves in trees or behind rocks, so as to have a cross-fire over the post in the centre of the glade.

This was immediately done. Goûmi and I took our

places in the same tree. Hood and Fox perched themselves in two magnificent oaks opposite each other.

Kâlagani hid behind a high rock, which he could climb
if the danger became imminent.

The animal would be thus enclosed in a circle, from
which it could not escape. All the chances were
against it, although we were as yet reckoning on the
unforeseen.

We had now to wait.

We could still hear the hoarse bark of the dispersed
jackals in the neighbouring thickets, but they did not
dare to return.

Nearly an hour had thus passed, when the yelps suddenly ceased. Almost immediately two or three jackals
bounded out of the wood, and, darting across the glade,
disappeared in the thicker part of the forest.

A sign from Kâlagani, who was ready to climb his
rock, told us to be on our guard.

We guessed that the precipitate flight of the jackals
must have been caused by the approach of some savage
animal,—the tigress no doubt,—so that we were ready
to see her at any moment appear on one side or other of
the glade.

Our guns were all ready. Captain Hood and his man
held their weapons pointed at the place from which the
jackals had issued.

Very soon I saw a slight agitation among the upper
branches of the thicket. The snapping of dry wood was
also heard. Some animal was approaching, but slowly
and warily. Though evidently seeing nothing of the
hunters in wait among the branches, its instinct warned
it that the place was not quite safe. Certainly, unless
urged by hunger, and attracted by the smell of the beef,
it would not have ventured further.

At last we could see it through the branches, where it
stopped, probably mistrustful.

It was a huge tigress, powerful and active. She began
to advance, crouching, and with an undulatory movement.

With one consent, we allowed her to approach the post. She smelt the ground, she drew herself up and arched her back, like a gigantic cat, prepared to spring.

Suddenly two sharp reports rang out.

" Forty-two ! " cried Captain Hood.

" Thirty-eight ! " shouted Fox.

The captain and his man had fired at the same moment, and with such true aim, that the animal, shot through the heart, fell dead on the ground.

Kâlagani ran up. We all quickly descended from our various trees.

The tigress did not stir.

But to whom belonged the honour of having killed her ? To the captain or to Fox ? This was an important question, as may be imagined.

The beast was examined. Two balls were found in the heart !

" Come," said Hood, not without a slight touch of regret in his voice, " we've got half a tiger apiece."

" So we have, captain ; half a tiger apiece," answered Fox, in the same tone.

And I verily believe neither of the two would, on any account, have given up the share he reckoned to his own account.

Such was this wonderful shot, of which the clearest result was that the animal had fallen without a struggle, and consequently without danger to the assailants,—a very rare occurrence.

Fox and Goûmi remained on the field of battle, in order to despoil the animal of her magnificent skin, whilst Captain Hood and I returned to Steam House.

It is not my intention to note every incident of our expeditions into the Terrai forest, but only those which present some particular characteristic. I shall content myself with saying that, so far, Captain Hood and Fox had had no reason to complain.

On the 20th of July, during a houddi hunt, a happy chance again favoured them, without their running any

D

real danger. The houddi, or hut, its walls pierced with loop-holes, is built on the borders of a stream at which animals are accustomed to come and drink. Used to the sight of these erections, they are not alarmed, and carelessly expose themselves to be shot at. But, to be safe, it is necessary to mortally wound the creature at the first, or he becomes dangerous, for the hut does not always protect the hunter from his infuriated spring.

This is exactly what occurred on the occasion of which I am about to speak. Mathias van Guitt accompanied us. Perhaps he hoped that some tiger, slightly wounded, might fall to his share, to take home to his kraal and be cured.

This time our sportsmen had three tigers to deal with, but the first discharge was not sufficient to prevent them from springing on to the walls of the houddi. The two first, to the zoologist's great disgust, were killed by a second ball, but the third leaped right in, his shoulder covered with blood, but not mortally wounded.

"We must have that fellow!" cried Van Guitt, who risked not a little in speaking thus. "We must take him alive!"

Scarcely had he uttered the words when, with a bound, the animal was upon him. He was overthrown in an instant, and it would have been all up with our friend had not Captain Hood sent a ball through the tiger's head, and thus saved the Dutchman, who sprang up, exclaiming,—

"Well, captain, you might just as well have waited—"

"Waited—what for?" answered Captain Hood; "until that brute had torn you to bits with his claws?"

"A wound with a claw needn't be mortal!"

"All right," returned Captain Hood quietly. "Another time I will wait!"

The tiger, however, instead of figuring in a menagerie, was fated only to be used as a hearthrug; but it brought up the list to forty-two for the captain, and thirty-eight for his man, without counting the half-tigress.

It must not be imagined that these grand hunts made us neglect smaller ones. Monsieur Parazard could not allow that. Antelopes, chamois, great bustards, of which there were numbers around Steam House, partridges and hares supplied our table with a great variety of game.

When we went into the Terrai, it was very rarely that Banks accompanied us.

Although these expeditions began to interest me, he did not seem to care for them. The upper zones of the Himalayas evidently offered him greater attractions, and he took pleasure in these excursions, especially when Colonel Munro consented to join him.

But it was only once or twice that the engineer could persuade his friend to do so. We observed that since our installation in the sanatarium, Sir Edward Munro had again become anxious. He spoke less, he kept aloof from us, but held long conferences with Sergeant McNeil. Were these two men meditating some new project which they wished to keep concealed even from Banks?

On the 13th of July Mathias van Guitt came to pay us a visit. Less favoured than the captain, he had not added a single fresh tenant to his menagerie. Neither tigers, lions, nor leopards seemed disposed to be caught. The idea of going to exhibit themselves in the countries of the West apparently did not allure them. Consequently the zoologist was in a very bad humour, and did not seek to hide it.

Kâlagani and two shikarrees accompanied him on this visit. The situation of our house pleased him much. Colonel Munro begged him to remain and dine. He consented with pleasure to honour our table.

Whilst waiting for dinner, Van Guitt wished to go over Steam House, the comfort of which was a contrast to the modest arrangements of the kraal. Our dwellings drew forth many compliments from him, but I must confess that Behemoth did not excite his admiration in

the least.   A naturalist, such as he was, could not but be
indifferent to this masterpiece of mechanics.   Re-
markable as it was, how could he admire a mere imitation
—a mechanical creation?

"Do not think badly of our elephant, Mr. van Guitt!"
said Banks.   "He is a powerful animal, who would
make nothing of drawing all your menagerie cages and
our cars as well."

"I have my buffaloes," answered the naturalist, "and
I prefer their slow and steady pace."

"Behemoth fears neither the claws nor teeth of
tigers!" cried Hood.

"No doubt, gentlemen," replied Mathias van Guitt,
"but why should wild beasts attack him?   They would
not care for iron flesh!"

Though the zoologist did not conceal his indifference
to our elephant, his men, and Kâlagani in particular,
were never tired of staring at it.   Mingled with their
admiration for the gigantic animal, there was evidently
some superstitious respect.   Kâlagani appeared very
much surprised when the engineer repeated that our
iron elephant was more powerful than all the teams at
the kraal put together.   This was an opportunity for
Captain Hood to describe, not without pride, our adventure with the three "proboscidate animals" belonging
to Prince Gourou Singh.   A slight incredulous smile
curled the lip of the naturalist, but he said nothing

Dinner passed off excellently well.   Van Guitt did
great justice to it.   The larder had been well supplied
with the product of our last excursion, and monsieur
certainly surpassed himself.

The cellar of Steam House was well stocked with
various liquors, which our guest much appreciated,
especially some French wines, after imbibing which his
matchless tongue wagged faster than ever.

So well did he relish them, that when we rose from
the table, to judge by his uncertain mode of progression, it was evident that if the wine had gone to his
head, it had also gone down into his legs.

Evening came on, and at last we separated, the best friends in the world, Mathias van Guitt, with the aid of his attendants, reaching his kraal in safety.

On the 16th of July something occurred which made a regular quarrel between the zoologist and the captain.

Hood shot a tiger just as it was about to enter one of the traps ; and though this made his forty-third, it was not the eighth which the purveyor wished for.

However after a lively interchange of epithets, harmony was once more restored, thanks to Colonel Munro's intervention, and Captain Hood promised to respect any animal who "had intentions" of being caught in Van Guitt's traps.

For the ensuing days the weather was detestable. We were obliged to stay indoors *nolens volens.* We were anxious that the rainy season should come to an end, and that could not now be long, for it had already lasted for more than three months. If the programme of our journey was carried out as Banks had arranged, we had only six weeks to pass in our sanatarium.

On the 23rd of July some hillmen came to pay a second visit to Colonel Munro. Their village, called Souari, lay but five miles from our encampment on the upper limit of the Terrai.

One of them told us, that for several weeks past, a tigress had been making frightful ravages on this part of the territory. The flocks were being carried off, and they even talked of abandoning Souari as uninhabitable. There was no safety in it, either for man or beast. Snares and traps had been tried without any success on the ravenous beast, which already was spoken of as one of the most formidable ever known among even the oldest mountaineers.

It may be guessed that the story excited Captain Hood at once. He immediately offered to accompany the men back to their village, ready to put his hunting experience and his accurate aim at the service of these honest people, who, I imagine, counted not a little on such an offer.

"Shall you come, Maucler?" asked the captain, in the tone of a man who did not wish to influence a determination.

"Certainly," I replied. "I should not like to miss such an interesting expedition."

"I will join you, this time," said the engineer.

"That's capital, Banks."

"Yes, Hood. I have a great wish to see you at work!"

"Am I not to go, captain?" asked Fox.

"Ah, you rascal!" laughed his master. "You won't be sorry for an opportunity to make up your half-tigress! Yes, Fox, yes, you shall go!"

As we should probably be absent from Steam House for three or four days, Banks asked the colonel whether he would not like to go with us to the village of Souari.

Sir Edward thanked him, but said he proposed to profit by our absence to visit the middle zone of the Himalayas above the belt of forest, with Goûmi and Sergeant McNeil.

Banks did not urge the matter.

It was decided that we should set out directly for the kraal, in order to borrow from Mathias van Guitt a few of his shikarrees, who might be useful to us.

About midday we arrived there, and acquainted the naturalist with our intentions. He could not conceal his secret satisfaction in hearing of the exploits of this tigress, "well calculated," said he, "to heighten the reputation of these felidæ of the peninsula in the minds of connoisseurs." He then placed at our disposal three of his men, besides Kâlagani, always ready for any danger.

It was settled with Captain Hood that, if by any possibility the tigress should be taken living, it was to belong to Van Guitt's menagerie. What an attraction it would be to have a placard hung in front of its cage, stating in eloquent terms the great deeds of "one of the Queens of the Terrai, who has devoured no less than a hundred and thirty-eight persons of both sexes!"

Our little band left the kraal about two o'clock in the afternoon. Before four o'clock, after ascending in an easterly direction, we arrived without adventure at Souari

The panic here was at its height.

That very morning a native had been surprised by the tigress near a stream and carried off into the forest.

We were received most hospitably in the house of a well-to-do farmer, an Englishman.

Our host had had more reason than any one else to complain of the savage beast, and would willingly pay several thousand rupees for its skin.

" Several years ago, Captain Hood," he said, " a tigress obliged the inhabitants of thirteen villages of the central provinces to take to flight, and in consequence a hundred and fifty miles were forced to lie fallow ! Well, if that sort of thing takes place here the whole province will have to be deserted ! "

" Have you employed every possible means to get rid of this tigress ? " asked Banks.

" Yes, indeed, everything ; traps, pitfalls, and even baits prepared with strychnine ! Nothing has succeeded ! "

" Well, my friend," said Captain Hood, " I can't promise for certain to give satisfaction, but I assure you we will do our very best."

Thereupon a battue was organized for that same day. Our party and the shikarrees were joined by about twenty mountaineers, who were well acquainted with the country.

Although Banks was so little of a sportsman, he accompanied our expedition with the most lively interest.

For three days we searched about all round the neighbourhood, but with no result, except that a couple of tigers, which no one thought much of, fell by the captain's gun.

" Forty-five ! " was all the remark he made.

At last the tigress signalized herself by a fresh misdeed. A buffalo, belonging to our host, disappeared from its pasture, and its remains were found about a quarter of a mile from the village. The assassination—premeditated murder, as a lawyer would say—had been accomplished before daybreak. The assassin could not be far off.

But was the principal author of this crime indeed the tigress so long sought in vain?

The natives of Souari had no doubt of it.

"I know it was my uncle, he did the mischief!" said one of the villagers to us.

"My uncle" is the natives' usual name for the tiger, they believing that the soul of each of their ancestors is lodged for eternity in the body of some member of the cat tribe. On this occasion it would certainly have been more correct to say "My aunt!"

It was immediately decided that we should set out in quest of the animal without waiting for night, as the darkness would conceal it more effectually than ever. We knew it must be gorged, and would probably not leave its den for two or three days.

We took the field. Starting from the place where the buffalo had been seized, traces of blood showed the direction the tigress had taken. These marks led us towards a thicket, which had been beaten many times already, without discovering anything. It was resolved to surround this spot so as to form a circle through which the animal could not escape, at least without being seen.

The villagers dispersed themselves around, so as to gradually narrow the circle. Captain Hood, Kâlagani, and I were on one side, Banks and Fox on the other, but in constant communication with the rest of the people. Each point of the ring was dangerous, since the tigress might try to break through anywhere.

There was no doubt that the animal was in this thicket, for the traces which entered one side did not reappear on the other. This did not prove though that it was its habitual retreat, for it had been searched before, but the presumptions were that it was its present refuge.

It was early, only eight o'clock. When all arrangements were made, we began to advance noiselessly, contracting the investing circle. In half an hour we were at the limit of the first trees.

Nothing had occurred, nothing had announced the presence of any creature, and for my own part I began to question whether we were not wasting our time.

Each could now only see the men next him, and yet it was important that we should advance with perfect unanimity. It had been previously agreed that the man who first entered the wood should fire a shot.

The signal was given by Captain Hood, who was always first in everything, and the border was crossed. I looked at my watch; it was thirty-five minutes past eight.

In a quarter of an hour the circle had so drawn in that our elbows touched, but we still had seen nothing.

Till now the silence had been unbroken, except by the snapping of dry branches under our feet.

Suddenly a roar was heard.

"The beast is in there!" cried Captain Hood, pointing to the mouth of a cavern in a mass of rocks and trees.

He was not mistaken. If it was not the usual haunt of the tigress, it was evidently her refuge now.

Hood, Banks, Fox, Kâlagani, and several other men approached the narrow opening to which the bloody traces led.

"We shall have to go in there," said the captain.

"A dangerous job!" remarked Banks. "It will be a serious matter for the first who enters!"

"I shall go in though," returned Hood, looking carefully to his rifle.

"After me, captain!" put in Fox, who was already stooping to enter the cave.

"No, no, Fox!" cried Hood. "This is my affair!"

"Ah, captain!" said Fox, in most persuasive yet reproachful accents, "I am six behind you!"

Just imagine their reckoning up their tigers at such a moment!

"Neither one nor the other shall enter ¡' exclaimed
Banks. "No! I can't allow it"

"There is another way," interrupted Kâlagani.

"What is that?"

"To smoke her out," replied the native. "She will
be forced to appear then. It will be easier and less
risky to kill her outside."

"Kâlagani is right," said Banks. "Come, my men,
dead wood, dry grass! Stop up the opening partly, so
that the wind may drive the smoke and flame inside.
The beast must either be roasted or run away!"

"It will run away," said the native.

"So much the better!" remarked Captain Hood.
"We shall be ready to give her a salute on her
way."

In a few minutes branches, grass, and dead wood, of
which there was plenty lying near, were piled in a heap
before the entrance to the den.

Nothing had stirred inside. Nothing could be seen
in the gloomy depths. Yet our ears could not have
deceived us, the roar certainly came from that place.

A light was set to the heap, and soon the whole was
in a blaze. From this bonfire issued a thick, choking
smoke, blowing right into the interior.

A second roar, more furious than the first, burst forth.
The creature was being driven to extremities, and would
make a rush.

We all waited anxiously, our faces towards the rocks,
and partially sheltered by the trees, so as to avoid the
first infuriated spring.

The captain had chosen another position, which, to
suit him, must, of course, be the most perilous. This was
in a gap between the brushwood, the only one which
offered a passage from the den. There Hood knelt on
one knee, so as to steady his aim, his rifle at his shoulder,
and looking as if carved in marble.

Three minutes had passed since the fire was first
lighted, when a third roar, a stifled, suffocated roar,

was heard. A huge monster dashed through the fire
and smoke!   The tigress at last!

"Fire!" shouted Banks.

Ten shots rang out, though we found afterwards that
not one had touched the animal.

Amid volumes of smoke, a second and yet longer
bound carried the animal towards the thicket.

Captain Hood, who waited with the greatest coolness,
fired, hitting her below the shoulder.

Like a lightning flash the tigress was upon him; over
he went, and in another moment her terrible claws would
have torn open his head.

But Kâlagani sprang forward, knife in hand.

In an instant the brave fellow had seized the tigress
by the throat.   The animal on this sudden attack shook
off the native, and turned upon him.

Feeling himself free, the captain leaped up, and
grasping the knife which had fallen from Kâlagani's
hand, plunged it into the creature's very heart.

The tigress rolled over.

This exciting scene had taken place in less time than
it takes to write it.

"Bag mahryaga! Bag mahryaga!" shouted the
natives,—meaning, "the tigress is dead!"

Yes, quite dead! But what a magnificent animal!
Ten feet from muzzle to tail, tall in proportion, and its
enormous paws armed with long claws, which looked as
if they had been sharpened up on a grindstone!

Whilst we were admiring the creature, the natives, who
had good reason for the grudge they bore against it,
overwhelmed it with invectives.

Kâlagani approached Captain Hood.

"I thank you, sahib!" he said.

"What are you thanking me for?" cried Hood.   "It's
I who owe you thanks, my brave fellow! If it hadn't
been for you, I should have been done for!"

"I should have been killed without your help!
replied the man coldly.

"What! By Jove—didn't you rush forward, knife in hand, to stab the tigress just as she was going to tear my skull open!"

"You killed him though, sahib, and that makes your forty-sixth!"

"Hurrah! hurrah!" cried the natives. "Hurrah for Captain Hood!"

The captain had certainly every right to add this tigress to his list, but he gave Kâlagani a grateful shake of the hand.

"Come to Steam House," said Banks to the man. "Your shoulder has been torn, and is bleeding; but we will find something in our medicine-chest to heal the wound."

Kâlagani acquiesced, and so, having taken leave of the inhabitants of Souari, who loaded us with thanks, we all proceeded in the direction of our sanatarium.

The shikarrees now left us, to return to the kraal. Again they went back empty-handed, and if Mathias van Guitt had counted on this "Queen of the Terrai," he must mourn for her; under the circumstances it was utterly impossible to take her alive.

We reached Steam House about midday.

Here unexpected news awaited us. To our extreme disappointment Colonel Munro, Sergeant McNeil, and Goûmi had gone away.

A note addressed to Banks told us not to be uneasy at their absence; that Sir Edward was desirous of re-connoitring the Nepaulese frontier, so as to clear up certain suspicions relating to the companions of Nana Sahib, but that he would return before the time at which we had arranged to leave the Himalayas.

On hearing this note read, I fancied that an involuntary movement denoting vexation escaped Kâlagani.

What could have occasioned this? I was mistaken, no doubt.

CHAPTER V.

A NIGHT ATTACK.

THE colonel's unexpected departure made us seriously uneasy. He was evidently still brooding over past events. But what could we do? Follow Sir Edward? We were ignorant of the direction he had taken, or even what point of the Nepaulese frontier he wished to reach.

On the other hand, we would not conceal from ourselves that as he had said nothing to Banks about this plan, it was because he dreaded his friend's expostulations and wished to avoid hearing them. Banks much regretted having followed us on our expedition.

All we could do now was to resign ourselves and wait.

Colonel Munro would certainly return before the end of August, that month being the last we were to pass in the sanatarium before proceeding south-west by the road to Bombay.

Kâlagani, who was well doctored by Banks, only remained four-and-twenty hours in Steam House. His wound began to heal rapidly, and he left us, to return to his duties at the kraal.

The month of August was ushered in by violent rains —weather bad enough to give a frog a cold in its head, as Captain Hood remarked; but as there was less wet than in July, it was consequently more propitious for our excursions into the Terrai.

Intercourse with the kraal was frequent. Mathias van Guitt continued dissatisfied. He, too, hoped to leave his camp in the beginning of September; but a lion, two tigers, and two leopards were still wanting, and he needed them to complete his troupe.

By way of retaliation, instead of the actors which he wished to engage on his employers' account, others came and presented themselves at his agency, for whom he had no occasion.

Thus, on the 4th of August, a fine bear was caught in one of his traps.

We happened to be in the kraal when the shikarrees brought back a cage containing a prisoner of great size, with black fur, sharp claws, and long hairy ears, which is a speciality of the ursine family in India.

"Now what do I want with this useless tardigrade ?" exclaimed the naturalist, shrugging his shoulders.

"Brother Ballon! Brother Ballon!" repeated the shi-karrees. Apparently though the natives are only nephews of tigers, they are the brothers of bears.

But Mathias van Guitt, notwithstanding this degree of relationship, received Brother Ballon with a very evident show of ill-humour. It certainly did not please him to catch bears when he wanted tigers. What was he to do with this inconvenient beast? It did not suit him to feed the animal without hopes of making any-thing by it. The Indian bear is little in request in the European market. It has not the mercantile value of the American grizzly, nor the Polar bear. Therefore Mathias van Guitt, being a good business-man, did not care to possess a cumbersome brute which he might find it very difficult to get rid of.

"Will you have him ?" asked he of Captain Hood.

"What on earth do you expect me to do with him ?" returned the captain.

"You can make him into beefsteaks," replied the zoologist, "if I may make use of the catachresis !"

"Mr. van Guitt," said Banks gravely, "the catachresis is allowable, when, for lack of any other expression, it renders the thought properly."

"That is quite my opinion," replied the zoologist.

"Well, Hood," said Banks, "will you, or will you not, take Mr. van Guitt's bear?"

"Of course not," replied the captain. "To eat bear-steaks when once the bear is killed, is all very well ; but to kill a bear on purpose to make steaks of him isn't an appetizing job!"

"Then you may give that plantigrade his liberty," said Van Guitt, turning to his shikarrees.

They obeyed. The cage was brought out of the kraal. One of the men opened the door.

Brother Ballon, who seemed rather ashamed of the situation, did not require to be asked twice. He walked calmly out of the cage, shook his head, which might be interpreted as meaning thanks, and marched off, uttering a grunt of satisfaction.

"That is a good deed you have performed," said Banks. "It will bring you luck, Mr. van Guitt!"

Banks was right enough. On the 6th of August the zoologist was rewarded by procuring one of the animals he wished for.

These are the circumstances of the capture : Mathias van Guitt, Captain Hood, and I, accompanied by Fox, Storr, and Kâlagani, had been beating a thicket of cactus and lentisks since daybreak, when a half-stifled roar was heard.

With our guns ready cocked, and walking near together, so as to guard against an isolated attack, we proceeded immediately to the suspected spot.

Fifty paces off the naturalist made us halt. He appeared to recognize the animal by the nature of the roar, and addressing himself more particularly to Captain Hood,—

"No useless firing, I beg," he whispered.

Then advancing a few steps, whilst we, obeying his sign, remained behind,—

"A lion!" he cried.

There indeed, at the end of a strong rope fastened to the forked branch of a tree, an animal was struggling.

The fierce beast, hanging by one of its fore-paws, which was tight in the slip-knot of the rope, gave terrible jerks without managing to free itself.

Captain Hood's first impulse in spite of Van Guitt's request, was to make ready to fire.

"Do not fire, captain!" exclaimed the naturalist. "I conjure you not to fire!"

"But—"

"No, no; I tell you! That lion is caught in one of my own snares, and he belongs to me!"

It was indeed a gallows-snare, at once simple and very ingenious.

A very strong rope is fixed to the branch of a tree, which is both tough and flexible. This branch is then bent down to the ground, so that the lower end of the cord, terminating in a running loop, hangs in a notch cut in a stake fixed firmly in the ground. On this stake is placed a bait, in such a position that if any animal wishes to get at it, he must put either his head or one of his paws in the noose. But as soon as he does this, and moves the bait ever so slightly, the cord is disengaged from the stake, the branch flies up, the animal is raised, and at the same moment a heavy cylinder of wood, sliding along the rope, falls on the knot, fixing it tightly and rendering vain all the efforts of the suspended animal to get free.

This species of snare is frequently set in the Indian forests, and wild animals allow themselves to be caught in them far more frequently than one would be tempted to believe. It usually happens that the beast is seized by the neck, causing almost immediate strangulation, while at the same time the skull is half fractured by the heavy wooden cylinder. But the lion which was now struggling before our eyes had only been caught by the paw. He was decidedly "all alive and kicking," as Captain Hood remarked, and well worthy to figure among the zoologist's guests.

Mathias van Guitt, in high delight, at once despatched

Kâlagani to the kraal, with orders to bring a cage in charge of a driver. Whilst he was gone we had ample leisure and opportunity to observe the captive, whose fury was redoubled by our presence.

The naturalist never took his eyes off him.

He walked round and round the tree, taking good care, however, to keep out of reach of the claws which the poor lion struck out in every direction.

In half an hour's time the cage appeared, drawn by two buffaloes. The suspended animal was cut down, not without some trouble, and we took the road to the kraal.

"Truly I was beginning to despair," said Van Guitt. "Lions do not figure in great numbers among the nemoral beasts of India."

"Nemoral?" said Captain Hood.

"Yes, beasts which haunt forests, and I have reason to congratulate myself on capturing this animal, which will do honour to my menagerie."

Dating from this day, Mathias van Guitt had no further reason to complain of ill-luck.

On the 11th of August two leopards were taken together in that first trap from which we liberated the naturalist. These creatures were cheetahs, similar to the one which so audaciously attacked Behemoth on the plains of Rohilkund, and which we were not able to shoot.

Two tigers only were now required to complete Van Guitt's stock.

It was now the 15th of August. Colonel Munro had not yet reappeared, and we had not received any news of him. Banks was more uneasy than he cared to show. He interrogated Kâlagani, who knew the Nepaul frontier, as to the danger Sir Edward might run by venturing into these independent territories.

The native assured him that not one of Nana Sahib's partisans remained within the confines of Thibet. However, he seemed to regret that the colonel had not chosen him for a guide. His services would have been very

P.

useful in a country with every path of which he was well acquainted. But there was no use now in thinking of joining him.

In the meanwhile Captain Hood and Fox more especially continued their excursions in the Terrai. Aided by the shikarrees, they contrived to kill three more tigers of medium size, not without great risk. Two of the animals went to the captain's account, the third to his man.

"Forty-eight!" said Hood, who greatly longed to make up the round number of fifty before quitting the Himalayas.

"Thirty-nine!" said Fox, without counting a formidable panther which had fallen by his gun.

On the 20th of August the last but one of the tigers wanted by Van Guitt was found in one of the pits, which either by instinct or chance the creatures had till then escaped. As is usually the case, the animal was hurt in its fall, but the injury was not serious. A few days' rest was sufficient to effect a cure, so that there would be nothing visible when delivery was made to Messrs. Hagenbeck, of Hamburg.

The use of this pit is regarded by connoisseurs as a barbarous method. When it is merely a question of destroying the animals, any way is good; but when it is necessary to take them alive, death is too often the consequence of their fall, especially when they are precipitated into a pit fifteen or twenty feet deep, destined for the capture of elephants. Out of ten there may be only one without some mortal injury. Therefore, even in Mysore, the naturalist told us, where the plan was at first so highly extolled, they are now beginning to give it up.

Mathias van Guitt, being anxious to set out for Bombay, did all in his power to obtain his last tiger.

It was not long before he had it in his possession, but at what a price! This incident deserves a detailed account, for the animal was dearly—too dearly—bought.

An expedition had been arranged by Captain Hood for the evening of the 26th of August. Circumstances combined to render it a favourable opportunity—a cloudless sky, a calm, still night, and a waning moon. When the darkness is very profound, wild beasts do not care to quit their lairs, but a half-light attracts them. Thus the meniscus—a word which Mathias van Guitt applied to the crescent moon—shed a few faint beams after midnight.

Captain Hood and I, Fox and Storr, who had taken a liking for the chase, formed the nucleus of this expedition, which was joined by the zoologist, Kâlagani, and a few of the natives.

Dinner ended, after taking leave of Banks, who had declined accompanying us, we left Steam House about seven in the evening, and at eight reached the kraal, without having met with any misadventure.

Mathias van Guitt was just finishing his supper. He received us in his usual demonstrative style. A council of war was held, and a plan agreed upon.

It was thought advisable to lie in wait at the edge of a stream falling down one of those ravines called "nullahs," a couple of miles from the kraal, at a place which a pair of tigers visited every night. No bait had been placed at this spot, as the natives pronounced it useless. A battue recently made in that part of the Terrai proved that the need to quench their thirst was sufficient to attract the tigers to the bottom of that nullah. They also said that it would be easy for us to post ourselves advantageously there.

As we were not to leave the kraal before midnight, and it was then but eight o'clock, we had to wait with what patience we might until the hour for departure.

"Gentlemen," said Mathias van Guitt, "my habitation is entirely at your disposal. I invite you to do as I intend doing, lie down and endeavour to obtain some sleep. We shall have to rise more than early, and a few hours' slumber will do much to fit us for our exertions."

"Do you care to have snooze, Maucler?" asked Captain Hood.

"No, thanks," I answered; "and I would rather keep myself awake by walking about than be roused out of my first sleep."

"Just as you please, gentlemen," answered the zoologist. "As for myself, I already feel that spasmodic winking of the eyelid which is caused by the need of sleep. You see I have already the pendulum movement!"

And Mathias van Guitt, raising his arms and throwing back his head and body, gave vent to several portentous yawns.

Then making us a profound bow, he retired into his hut, and was doubtless soon fast asleep.

"Now what are we going to do?" asked I.

"Let us walk about, Maucler," answered Captain Hood, "up and down in the kraal. It is a fine night, and I shall feel much more fit for a start than if I had three or four hours' nap first. Besides, though sleep is called our best friend, it is a friend who often keeps us waiting!"

We were now strolling up and down in the enclosure, thinking or chatting as we chose. Storr, "whose best friend was not likely to keep him waiting," was already asleep, lying at the foot of a tree. The shikarrees and the rest were all crouched in their several corners, and no one in the place was awake but ourselves.

Keeping a watch would have been useless, as the kraal was entirely surrounded by a close and solid palisade.

Kâlagani himself made sure that the door was securely fastened; then, that duty performed, he wished us goodnight as he passed and joined his companions.

Captain Hood and I were absolutely alone.

Not only Van Guitt's people, but the domestic animals and wild beasts were equally reposing, the first in groups under the trees at one end of the kraal, the latter in their cages. Perfect silence reigned within and without.

Our stroll took us first to the place occupied by the buffaloes. These magnificent ruminants, quiet and docile, were not even tethered. Accustomed to repose under the shade of gigantic maples, there they lay, their great horns entangled, their feet folded beneath them, and deep sonorous breathing issuing from their enormous bodies. Even our approach did not arouse them. One only lifted his huge head for a moment, and looked sleepily at us, but soon put it down again.

"See to what a state tameness, or rather domestication, has reduced them," I remarked.

"Yes," replied Hood; "and yet buffaloes are terrible animals when in a savage state. But though they are so strong, they have not agility, and what can their horns do against the teeth and claws of lions and tigers? The advantage is decidedly on the side of the latter."

Talking thus, we approached the cages. There, too, all was still. Tigers, lions, panthers, leopards, all were asleep in their various compartments. Mathias van Guitt wisely did not put them together until they were somewhat tamed by a few weeks of captivity. Otherwise the brutes would most certainly have eaten each other up the very first day.

The three lions crouched motionless in a half-circle, like huge cats. Nothing of their heads could be seen, so buried were they in a thick muff of black fur, and they slept the sleep of the just.

Slumber was less profound in the tigers' apartment. Their glowing eyes flamed through the dusk. Now and again a great paw would be stretched out, clawing at the iron bars. This was the sleep of fretful and impatient carnivora.

"They are having bad dreams, and I feel for them!" said the compassionate captain.

Some remorse, no doubt, troubled the three panthers, or at least some regret. At this hour, in their free life, they would have been roaming through the forest! They would have prowled around the pastures in quest of living flesh.

As to the four leopards, no nightmare disturbed their rest. They reposed peacefully. Two of these felines, a male and female, occupied the same room, being to all appearance as comfortable as if they were in their own den.

A single compartment was still empty—the one destined for the sixth and impracticable tiger, for whose capture Mathias van Guitt yet lingered in the Terrai.

Our promenade had lasted for nearly an hour. After once more making the tour of the kraal, we seated ourselves at the foot of an enormous mimosa.

Absolute silence reigned over the entire forest. The wind, which whistled through the trees as night fell, had now died away. Not a leaf rustled.

Captain Hood and I, now seated near each other, no longer chatted. Not that we were becoming drowsy. It was rather that sort of absorption, more moral than physical, which is the effect produced by the perfect repose of nature. One thinks without forming the thought. One dreams as a man dreams without sleeping, when the wide open eyes gaze far away, seeing only some vision of the fancy.

One peculiarity surprised the captain, and unconsciously speaking in an undertone, as if fearing to break the silence, he said,—

"Maucler, this stillness astonishes me! Generally there are wild beasts roaring all night and making the forest a most noisy place. If not tigers or panthers, at any rate the jackals never rest. This kraal, full of living beings, ought to attract hundreds of them, and yet we hear nothing, not a snap of dry wood, or even a howl. If Mathias van Guitt was awake, he would wonder as much as I do, no doubt, and would find some long break-jaw word by which to express his surprise!"

"Your observation is correct, my dear Hood," I replied; "and I do not know to what cause to attribute the absence of these night prowlers. But we must take care, or we shall end by going to sleep ourselves!"

"No, no, fight against it!" returned the captain, stretching himself. "It will soon be time for us to start."

And we continued to interchange sentences at somewhat long intervals.

How long this lasted I cannot say, but suddenly a noise was heard which quickly aroused me from my drowsy state. There was no doubt about it, the noise issued from the wild beasts' cage.

Lions, tigers, panthers, leopards, till now so peaceful, were uttering sullen growls of anger. Pacing up and down their narrow dens, they seemed to scent something afar off, and stopped every now and again to rear themselves up against the bars and sniff the air.

"What's the matter with them?" asked I.

"I don't know," answered Hood, "but I fear they scent the approach of—"

At that moment tremendous roars were heard outside the enclosure.

"Tigers!" exclaimed Hood, running towards Van Guitt's hut.

But such was the violence of the roaring that all the inhabitants of the kraal were already on foot, and the zoologist met him at the door.

"An attack?" he cried.

"I believe so," replied the captain.

"Stop! I will see!"

And without taking time to finish his phrase, Mathias van Guitt, seizing a ladder, placed it against the palisade. In a moment he was at the top.

"Ten tigers and a dozen panthers!" he cried.

"That's serious," answered Captain Hood. "We intended hunting them, and now they have come hunting us!"

"Your guns—get your guns!" cried the zoologist.

Obeying his orders, in half a minute we were ready to fire.

Attacks by a band of wild beasts are not rare in India. The inhabitants of districts infested by tigers, particularly the Sunderbunds, have often been besieged in their dwellings. This is a dreadful event, and too often the victory rests with the assailants.

In the meanwhile to the roars outside were joined howls and growls from the inside. The kraal was answering the forest. We could scarcely hear ourselves speak.

"To the palisades!" shouted Van Guitt, making us understand what he wanted more by his gestures than his voice.

We all hastened forward.

At that moment the buffaloes, a prey to the wildest terror, endeavoured to force their way out from their enclosure, while the men vainly tried to keep them back.

Suddenly the gate, having no doubt been insecurely fastened, was burst violently open, and a whole troop of wild beasts rushed in.

And yet Kâlagani was supposed to have closed that gate carefully ; he did so every evening !

"To the hut! to the hut!" shouted Van Guitt, running towards his house, which alone offered a refuge.

But should we have time to reach it ?

Already two shikarrees lay stretched on the earth. The others fled across the enclosure, seeking a shelter.

The zoologist, Storr, and six natives were already in the house, and closed the door just in time, as a couple of tigers were about to spring in.

Kâlagani, Fox, and the rest had caught hold of trees, and hoisted themselves up among the branches.

As for the captain and myself, we had no time nor opportunity for joining Van Guitt.

"Maucler! Maucler!" shouted Hood, whose right arm had just received a wound.

With a blow of his tail a huge tiger had thrown me to the ground. Before he had time to turn upon me, I rose and hastened to Captain Hood's assistance.

One refuge still remained to us ; the empty compartment of the sixth cage. We sprang in, and in a moment we had closed the door, and were for a time safe from the brutes, who threw themselves, growling savagely, against the iron bars.

Such was the fierceness of the furious beasts, joined to the anger of the tigers imprisoned in the neighbouring compartments, that the cage, oscillating on its wheels, seemed on the point of being capsized.

The tigers, however, soon abandoned it to attack some more certain prey.

What a scene it was ! not a detail of it was lost to us, looking through the bars of our cage.

"The world is turned upside down !" cried Hood, who was almost mad with vexation. "Those brutes to be out, and we shut up !"

"Your wound ?" I asked.

"That's nothing !"

Five or six shots were at this moment heard.

The firing was from the hut, around which two tigers and three panthers were raging.

One of the animals was killed by an explosive ball from Storr's rifle. The others retreated and fell upon the herd of buffaloes, who were utterly defenceless against such adversaries.

Fox, Kâlagani, and the natives, who had dropped their weapons in their haste to climb the trees, could give no assistance.

However, Captain Hood, taking aim between the bars of our cage, fired. Although his right arm, being almost paralyzed by his wound, prevented him from taking his usual unerring aim, he was lucky enough to "pot his forty-ninth tiger."

The buffaloes leaped from their enclosure, and rushed bellowing through the kraal. They vainly endeavoured to gore the tigers, who, however, easily kept out of reach of their horns.

One of them, mounted by a panther, his claws

tearing its neck, rushed out and away through the forest.

Five or six others, pursued closely by the beasts, also disappeared.

A few of the tigers followed; but the buffaloes who had not been able to escape lay slaughtered and torn on the ground.

Other shots were fired through the windows of the hut. But whilst Hood and I were doing our part, a new danger menaced us.

The animals shut up in the cages, excited by the rage of the struggle, the smell of blood, the roars of their brethren, rampaged about with indescribable violence. Would they end by breaking their bars? This seemed really likely. In fact, one of the tigers' cages was turned over. I thought for a moment that it would burst open and let them loose!

Fortunately nothing like this happened, and the prisoners could not even see what was passing outside, since it was the barred side of the cage which was downwards.

"Decidedly there are too many of them!" muttered the captain, as he reloaded.

At that moment, a tiger made a prodigious spring, and clung to the fork of a tree, on which two or three shikarrees had sought refuge.

One of the unfortunate men was seized and dragged down to the ground.

There a panther disputed with the tiger for the pos session of the dead body, crunching the bones in the midst of a sea of blood.

"Fire now! Why don't you fire?" shouted the captain, as if Van Guitt and his companions could hear him.

As to us, we could do nothing more. Our cartridges were exhausted, and we could only remain powerless spectators of the scene.

Even this did not last long; a tiger in the next compartment to ours, who had been endeavouring to break out, managed by giving a violent shake to destroy the equilibrium of the cage. It oscillated for a moment, and then over it went.

Slightly bruised by the fall, we soon scrambled again to our knees. The sides bore the shock, but now we could no longer see what was going on outside.

Though we could not see, we could at least hear! What a hideous din! What a horrid odour of blood! The fight seemed to have taken a still more violent character. What had happened? Had the prisoners in the other cages escaped? Were they attacking Van Guitt's hut? Were the tigers and panthers springing into the trees and tearing down the natives?

"And we all the time shut up in this abominable box!" exclaimed Captain Hood, wild with excitement and rage.

Nearly a quarter of an hour—which appeared whole hours to us—passed in this way.

Then the uproar began to calm down. The roaring and howling diminished. The bounds of the tigers which occupied the compartments in one cage were less frequent. Had the massacre come to an end?

All at once I heard the gate of the kraal slammed to with great noise, and Kâlagani's voice calling to us loudly, then Fox shouting,—

"Captain! captain!"

"This way!" cried Hood.

He was heard, and we soon felt the cage being lifted. A moment more and we were free.

"Fox! Storr!" called the captain, whose first thougdt was for his companions.

"Here, sir!" answered both the men.

They were not even wounded. Mathias Van Guitt and Kâlagani were equally safe and sound. Two tigers and a panther lay lifeless on the ground. The others had left the kraal, and Kâlagani had shut them out. We were all in safety. None of the beasts of the menagerie

had effected an escape during the combat, and, besides
that, the zoologist now counted one prisoner more. This
was a young tiger imprisoned in the small travelling
cage, which had upset over him, and under which he was
caught as in a snare.

The stock of Mathias van Guitt was thus completed ;
but it had cost him dear ! Five of his buffaloes were
killed ; and three of his natives, horribly mutilated,
weltered in their blood on the grass of the enclosure !

CHAPTER VI.

MATHIAS VAN GUITT'S FAREWELL.

DURING the rest of the night no other incident occurred either in or outside the kraal. The gate was securely fastened this time. How was it that at the very time the wild beasts surrounded the palisade it should have been open? This was truly most unaccountable, for Kâlagani had himself placed the strong bars which fastened it.

Captain Hood's wound gave him considerable pain, although it was but skin-deep. A little more though would have caused him to lose the use of his right arm.

For my part, I felt nothing of the violent blow which had thrown me to the ground.

We resolved to return to Steam House as soon as day began to dawn.

As to Mathias van Guitt, except for regretting the loss of three of his people, he was not at all disheartened, although the being deprived of his buffaloes must put him to some inconvenience when the time for his departure came.

"It is but the chances of the trade," he said, "and I have for long had a presentiment that an adventure of this kind would befall me."

He then proceeded to arrange for the interment of the three natives, whose remains were laid in a corner of the kraal in a grave deep enough to prevent any wild animals disturbing them.

Soon, however, the dawn began to light up the dark avenues of the Terrai, and after many shakes of the hand, we took leave of Mathias van Guitt. To accompany us on our walk through the forest the zoologist put at our disposal Kâlagani and two natives. His offer was accepted, and at six o'clock we left the kraal.

No untoward incident marked our return journey. Of tigers and panthers there was not a trace. The animals, having been so severely repulsed, had no doubt retreated to their dens, and this was not the time to go and rouse them up. As to the buffaloes which had escaped from the kraal, they had either been slain and devoured in the depths of the forest, or, if still alive, having fled to a great distance, it was not to be expected that their instinct would lead them back to the encampment. They must therefore be considered as positively lost to the naturalist.

At the border of the forest, Kâlagani and the other men left us, and not long after Fan and Niger welcomed us back with joyful barks to Steam House.

I recounted our adventures to Banks, and it is needless to say that he congratulated us heartily on having got off so well! Too often in attacks of this nature not one of the assailed party escapes to tell the tale of the exploits of the assailants!

As to Captain Hood, he was obliged, whether he liked it or not, to keep his arm in a sling; but the engineer, who was the doctor of the expedition, found his wound not serious, and declared that in a few days no trace of it would remain.

At heart Captain Hood was much mortified at having received a wound without having returned it. And yet he had added another tiger to the forty-eight already on his list.

On the afternoon of the 27th our attention was aroused by the joyful and excited barking of the dogs.

We hastened out and saw Colonel Munro, McNeil, and Goûmi. Their return was a real relief to us. Had Sir Edward succeeded in his expedition? This we did not yet know. He was there, however, safe and sound, and that was the most important thing after all.

Banks immediately hurried up to him, grasped his hand, and gave him a questioning look.

" Nothing ! " was all the reply he received, accompanied by a shake of the head.

This word signified not only that the search of the Nepaulese frontier had resulted in nothing, but that any conversation on this subject would be useless. It appeared to mean that there was nothing to speak about.

McNeil and Goûmi, whom Banks interrogated in the evening, were more explicit. They told him that Colonel Munro had indeed wished to survey that portion of Hindoostan in which Nana Sahib had taken refuge before his reappearance in the Bombay Presidency ; to ascertain what had become of the Nabob's companions ; to search for any traces which might remain of their passage over that part of the frontier ; to endeavour to learn whether, instead of Nana Sahib, his brother, Balao Rao, was hiding in that country. Such had been Sir Edward's object.

The result of this search was that there could no longer be any doubt that the rebels had left the country. There was not a vestige of that camp in which the false obsequies of Nana Sahib had been celebrated. No news was heard of Balao Rao ; of his companions, nothing that could urge them to set off on the track. The Nabob killed in the defiles of the Sautpoora Mountains, his friends probably dispersed beyond the limits of the peninsula, the work of the avenger seemed already performed. To quit the Himalayas, continue southwards, and thus finish our journey from Calcutta to Bombay, was all we had now to think of.

The departure was fixed for a week from that time, for the 3rd of September. That time was necessary to complete the healing of Captain Hood's wound. Colonel Munro too, who was plainly fatigued by his excursion through that rough country, was also glad of a few days' rest.

During this time Banks began his preparations by

getting our train in order and in a state for the journey from the Himalayas to Bombay.

To begin with, it was agreed that the route should be a second time altered, so as to avoid the great towns of the north-west, Mirat, Delhi, Agra, Gwalior, Jansi, and others, in which so many disasters of the mutiny of 1857 had taken place. With the last rebels of the insurrection had disappeared all that could arouse the recollections of Colonel Munro.

Our travelling dwelling would thus go straight through the provinces without stopping at the principal cities, but the country was well worth a visit, if only for its natural beauties. The immense kingdom of Scindia is un-equalled in this respect. The most picturesque roads in the peninsula now lay before Behemoth.

The season of the monsoons had ended with the rainy season, which is not prolonged beyond the month of August. The first days of September promised a most agreeable temperature, which would render the second part of our journey far pleasanter than the first.

During this last week of our stay in the sanatarium, Fox and Goûmi purveyed daily for the pantry. Accom-panied by the two dogs, they found swarms of partridges, pheasants, and bustards. These birds, preserved in the ice-house, were to supply us with game during the journey.

We paid two or three more visits to the kraal. There Mathias van Guitt was also preparing for his departure for Bombay, bearing his troubles with the philosophy which carried him calmly through all the miseries of existence, both great and small.

The capture of the tenth tiger had completed his stock. It was now only necessary to make up the number of his buffaloes. Not one of those which fled during the night attack had been recaptured. The chances were that all, dispersed in the forest, had met with violent deaths. The difficulty was how to make up the teams. In hopes of obtaining animals among the scattered farms and villages of the neighbourhood, Van Guitt had sent Kâlagani to inquire, and awaited his return with some impatience.

The last week of our abode at the sanatarium passed without incident. Captain Hood's wound gradually healed, and he seemed to hope for one more expedition before closing the campaign. But this idea Colonel Munro would not encourage.

Why risk himself needlessly while his arm was weak?

During the rest of our journey he would be very likely to meet with sport *en route*.

"Besides," observed Banks, "you surely ought to be satisfied to find yourself alive and well, with a score of forty-nine tigers fallen to your gun. The balance is all in your favour."

"Forty-nine—yes," returned the captain with a sigh ; "but I wanted fifty."

He was evidently dissatisfied.

The 2nd of September arrived and we were on the eve of departure.

In the morning Goûmi came in to announce a visit from the purveyor.

Van Guitt, accompanied by Kâlagani, came to Steam House ; no doubt he wished to take formal leave at the last moment.

Colonel Munro received him cordially, and the Dutchman plunged into a course of speechifying more astonishing than ever. It struck me that his high-flown compliments concealed something which he hesitated to propose.

Banks brought him to the point by inquiring whether he had succeeded in making up his buffalo teams.

"No, indeed, Mr. Banks," he replied, "Kâlagani has been unsuccessful. Although I gave him *carte blanche* as to price, he failed to procure a single pair of these useful animals. I am forced to admit myself wholly at a loss how to convey my menagerie to the nearest railway

F

station.   This loss of my buffaloes, by the sudden attack
on the night between the 25th and 26th of August, em-
barrasses me exceedingly.   My cages with their four-
footed prisoners are heavy, and—"

"Well, how are you going to manage?" demanded
the engineer.

"I can't exactly say," returned Mathias.   "I plan—I
contrive—I hesitate—but the fact is that on the 20th of
September, that is to say eighteen days hence, I am
bound to deliver the animals at Bombay."

"In eighteen days!" echoed Banks.   "Why, you have
not an hour to lose."

"I know it, sir, and I have but one resource, just one."

"What may that be?"

"It is to entreat the colonel to do me a very great
favour."

"Speak freely, Mr. van Guitt," said Colonel Munro;
"if I can oblige you, I will do so with pleasure."

Mathias bowed, placed his right hand on his lips,
swayed himself from side to side, and in every gesture betokened himself overwhelmed by unexpected
kindness.

He then explained that, understanding our giant
engine to be of immense power, he wished to know if it
would be possible to attach his caravan of cages to our
train, and so to drag them to Etawah, the nearest station
on the line between Delhi and Allahabad.

The colonel turned to the engineer, saying,—

"Can we do what Mr. van Guitt requires?"

"I see no difficulty," replied Banks.   "Behemoth will
never know that he draws a heavier weight."

"It shall be done, Mr. van Guitt," said Colonel Munro.
"We will take your goods to Etawah.   People ought to
be neighbourly and help one another even in the
Himalayas."

"I am aware of your goodness, colonel," replied Van
Guitt, "and indeed felt I might reckon on it."

"You were right," said Colonel Munro.

Everything being thus arranged, the Dutchman prepared to return to his kraal, in order to dismiss such of his attendants as were no longer required, retaining only four shikarrees who were wanted to tend the animals.

" We meet to-morrow, then," said Colonel Munro.

"To-morrow, gentlemen, I shall be ready, and waiting for you and your steam monster at my kraal."

And the purveyor, delighted with the success of his visit, retired with all the airs of an actor leaving the stage.

Kâlagani, after fixedly regarding Colonel Munro, whose journey to the frontiers of Nepaul appeared to interest him deeply, followed his master.

The last arrangements were completed. Everything was in travelling order, and of the Steam House sanatarium nothing remained.

We were ready to descend to the plains, where our elephant was to leave us and fetch the Dutchman's caravan to join our train, which then was to start across Rohilkund. At seven o'clock on the morning of the 3rd September, Behemoth stood ready to resume the duties he had hitherto so well fulfilled. But a very unexpected occurrence now excited the surprise of every one.

After lighting the furnace to heat the boiler, Kâlouth opened the different flues and the soot-doors, in order to be sure that nothing impeded the draught of air, but started back when, with a strange sound of hissing, a score of what seemed like leathern thongs darted towards him from the tubes.

" Hallo, Kâlouth! What's the matter ? " said Banks.

" A swarm of serpents, sahib," cried the stoker.

In fact, what appeared like straps were snakes which had chosen to make themselves at home in the furnace chimneys, whence the heat now dislodged them. Some were scorched, and fell to the ground ; had not Kâlouth opened the valves, all would speedily have been roasted.

" What ! " cried Captain Hood, running forward, " has

Behemoth been cherishing a brood of serpents in his bosom ? "

Yes, of the most dangerous and numerous description, and a superb tiger-python now showed his pointed head from the tip of the elephant's trunk, and began to unfold his coils, amid spiral volumes of smoke. The other serpents, which were so lucky as to escape with their lives, quickly vanished among the bushes.

But the python could not easily ascend the cast iron cylinder, and Captain Hood had time to get his rifle and send a bullet through its head.

Then Goûmi mounted the elephant, and scrambling up the trunk succeeded, with the help of Kâlouth and Storr, in hoisting out the huge reptile.

It was a most magnificent boa, in a vesture of gorgeous green and purple, adorned with regular rings, which seemed as though cut out of splendid tiger-skin. It was as thick as a man's arm, and measured quite five yards in length.

Truly it was a superb specimen, and would have made an advantageous addition to Van Guitt's collection, could it have been secured alive.

The excitement of this incident having subsided, Kâlouth rearranged his furnace, the boiler soon began to do its part, and steam being fairly got up, we were ready to be off.

One last glance over the marvellous panorama spread before us to the south, one last lingering look towards the indented outlines of the mighty mountain peaks which stood forth sharply against the northern sky, and then the shriek of the whistle gave notice of departure.

We descended the winding road without difficulty, the atmospheric brake acting admirably on the steep pitches, and in an hour we halted on the lower limit of the Terrai, at the edge of the plain.

Here Behemoth, under charge of Banks and the fireman, left us, and at a dignified pace entered one of the broad roads through the forest.

A couple of hours later we heard the snorting and puffing of the steam giant, and he issued from the thicket of trees with the Dutchman's caravan menagerie in tow.

Mathias van Guitt made his appearance, and renewed his thanks to the colonel. The wild-beast cages, with a van in front for the purveyor and his men, were attached to our train, now composed of eight carriages.

Banks gave the signal, the regulation whistle sounded, and Behemoth, with stately motion, began to advance along the magnificent road leading to the south. The addition of Van Guitt and his wild-beast vans made no difference to him.

" Well, Van Guitt, what do you think of it ? " inquired Captain Hood.

" I think, captain," replied Mathias, with some reason, "that this elephant would be much more wonderful if he were made of flesh and blood."

We did not follow the route by which we had reached the foot of the Himalayas, but travelled south-west towards the little town of Philibit. We went at a moderate and easy pace, and met with no hindrance or discomfort. The Dutchman daily took his seat at our table, when his splendid appetite never failed to do honour to the culinary talents of Monsieur Parazard.

It speedily became necessary to call upon our sports-men to do their duty, and Captain Hood resumed his labours for the larder.

Food was required for our four-footed passengers, as well as for ourselves, and the shikarrees took care to provide it. They were clever hunters ; and led by Kâlagani, himself a first-rate shot, kept up a supply of bison and antelope meat.

Kâlagani maintained his peculiar and reserved man-ners, although very kindly treated by Colonel Munro, who was not a man to forget a good service done him.

On the 10th of September our train skirted the town of Philibit without making a halt, but a considerable number of natives came to see us.

Van Guitt's wild-beast show attracted little attention in comparison with Behemoth, and without more than a passing glance at the splendid creatures within their cages, all hastened to admire the Steam Elephant.

We traversed the great plains of Northern India, passing, at a distance of some leagues, Bareilly, one of the chief cities of Rohilkund. Sometimes we were surrounded by forests filled with birds of brilliant plumage, sometimes by dense thickets of the thorny acacia two or three yards high, which is called by the English " Wait-a-bit."

There we met with many wild boars, whose flesh was of a remarkably fine flavour, from the fact of their feeding on the yellowish berry of these plants. These boars are extremely savage animals, and on several occasions they were killed by Captain Hood and Kâla-gani, under circumstances which displayed to advantage all the courage and skill possessed by our mighty hunters.

Between Philibit and Etawah railway station our train had to cross the Upper Ganges, and shortly after an important tributary, the Kali-Nacli.

The menagerie vans were detached, and Steam House, assuming its nautical character, easily floated from one bank to the other.

It was different with the Dutchman's vans. They had to be transported singly by a ferry boat, and, though tedious, the passage was effected without much difficulty, as both he and his men knew exactly what to do.

At length without any adventure worthy of notice we reached the line of rail between Delhi and Allahabad.

Here the two parts of our train were to separate, the first continuing to descend southwards across the vast territories of Scind, in order to reach the Vindhyas and the presidency of Bombay. The second was to be placed on railway trucks to travel to Bombay, and so by ship to Europe.

We encamped together for one night, and the respective starts were to be made at daybreak

Mathias van Guitt was about to dismiss such of his attendants as were no longer necessary to him, retaining the natives only until he should reach the ship.

Among the men now paid off was Kâlagani, the hunter.

We had become attached to this native since he had rendered good service both to Colonel Munro and Captain Hood, and Banks, perceiving him to be at a loss for employment, asked if it would suit him to accompany us as far as Bombay.

After some moments' consideration, Kâlagani accepted the proposal, which seemed to please Colonel Munro very much. He was well acquainted with all this part of India, and attached to the staff of Steam House was likely to be extremely useful to us.

The next morning the camp was struck. Steam was up, and Storr only awaited final orders.

The ceremony of leave-taking was very simple on our part, highly theatrical on that of Van Guitt, who amplified his expressions of thanks, and specially distinguished himself in the final scene, when, as he disappeared from our sight, he indicated by pantomimic gestures that never, either here below or in life hereafter, should our kindness fade from his memory.

CHAPTER VII.

PASSAGE OF THE BETTWA.

OUR position on the 18th of September stood thus,—

    Distance from Calcutta .   .   812 miles.

    From Sanatarium on the Himalayas   236 miles.

    From Bombay . . . . 1000 miles.

With regard to distance, not half of our proposed journey had been accomplished, but, reckoning the seven weeks spent on the Himalayan frontier, above half the time allotted to it had elapsed. We left Calcutta on the 6th of March, and in two months we hoped to reach the western shores of Hindostan.

Avoiding the great towns concerned in the revolt of 1857, we should travel nearly due south. There being excellent roads through Scind, we should meet no difficulties until we came to the mountains of Central India. The presence of an experienced man like Kâlagani would give additional security as well as facility to our progress, as he seemed so thoroughly well acquainted with this part of Hindostan.

Banks called him the first day, while Colonel Munro was taking his siesta, and asked in what capacity he had so frequently traversed these provinces.

"I belonged," replied the man, "to one of the numerous caravans of Brinjarees, who convey to the interior, on the backs of oxen, supplies of grain, either ordered by the government or private persons. In this capacity I have passed a score of times across the territories of North and Central India."

"Do such caravans still cross this part of the peninsula?"

"Yes, sir, they do, and at this season of the year I should expect to meet Brinjarees on their way north."

"Well, Kâlagani, you are likely to be very useful to us. We wish to avoid the great cities, and to pass through the open country. You shall be our guide."

"Certainly, sir," answered the Hindoo, in the cold tone which was habitual to him, and to which I could never get quite reconciled. Then he added, "Shall I state in a general way the direction we shall have to take?"

"Do so, Kâlagani," said Banks, spreading a large map on the table, and preparing to verify by observation the information about to be given him.

"It is very simple," said the Indian. "A direct line takes us from the Delhi railroad to that of Bombay. The junction is at Allahabad. Between Etawah and the frontier of Bundelkund there is but one important river to cross, the Jumna; between that and the Vindhyas mountains there is another, the Bettwa. These two rivers may have overflowed their banks, but I think your train would be able to cross them even if it were so."

"There would be no serious difficulty," replied the engineer. "And having reached the Vindhyas—?"

"We should turn slightly to the south-east, in order to reach a practicable pass. There will be no difficulty there either, for I know a spot where the ascents are easy. Wheel carriages prefer that way; it is the pass of Sirgour."

"That ought to suit us," returned Banks, "but I perceive that beyond the pass of Sirgour the country is very hilly. Could we not approach the Vindhyas by crossing Bhopal?"

"There are a great many towns in that direction," answered Kâlagani; "it would be difficult to avoid them. The sepoys distinguished themselves particularly there during the war of independence."

I was struck by this expression, "the war of independence," which Kâlagani applied to the mutiny. However, I reflected that it was a native, not an Englishman,

who used it.   Besides, we had no reason to suppose that
Kâlagani had taken part in the revolt.

"Well," resumed Banks, "leaving the cities of Bhopal
to the west, are you certain that the pass of Sirgour will
give us access to a practicable road?"

"To a road I have often travelled, sir, which, after
making the circuit of Lake Puturia, will bring you near
Jubbulpore, on the Bombay railway."

"I see," said Banks, who followed on the map all that
the man said; "and after that—?"

"After that the road turns to the south-west, and,
more or less, runs alongside the line as far as Bombay."

"Of course,—so it does," returned Banks. "I see no
particular difficulty anywhere, and the route suits us.
We shall not forget your services, Kâlagani."

Kâlagani made his salaam, and was about to retire,
when, changing his mind, he again approached the
engineer.

"Have you any question to put to me?" said Banks.

"I have, sir; may I be permitted to ask why you
especially want to avoid the great towns of the Bundelkund?"

Banks looked at me. There seemed no reason for
concealing the facts of the case from this man, and after
a little consideration Colonel Munro's position was
explained to him.

He listened attentively to what the engineer related
to him, and then he said in a tone denoting surprise,—

"Colonel Munro has nothing more to fear from Nana
Sahib—at least not in these provinces."

"Neither in these provinces nor anywhere else," returned Banks. "Why do you say 'in these provinces'?"

"Because it was reported several months ago that the
Nabob had reappeared in the Bombay Presidency, but
by no research could his retreat be discovered, and, supposing him ever to have been there, it is probable that
he has now again passed beyond the Indo-Chinese
frontier."

This answer seemed to prove that Kálagani was ignorant of what had taken place in the Sautpourra Mountains, and that in the month of May Nana S.hib had been slain by British soldiers at the Pâl of Tandit.

"It seems that news takes a long time to reach the Himalayan forests!" exclaimed Banks.

Kâlagani looked at him fixedly, like one not in the least comprehending his words.

"You do not seem to know that Nana Sahib is dead," continued the engineer.

"Nana Sahib dead!" cried the native.

"Certainly," replied Banks, "government announced the fact that he had been killed, with all the details."

"Killed?" said Kâlagani, shaking his head, "where do they say Nana Sahib was killed?"

"At the Pâl of Tandit, in the Sautpourra Mountains."

"And when?"

"Nearly four months ago, on the 25th of last May.

I noticed a peculiar look flit over Kâlagani's face as he folded his arms and remained silent.

"Have you any reason," inquired I, "for discrediting the account of Nana Sahib's death?"

"None, sir; I believe what you tell me."

In another instant Banks and I were alone, and he exclaimed, "You see what these fellows are! They regard the chief of the rebel sepoys as something more than mortal, and because they have not seen him hanged, they never will believe he is dead."

"Why," replied I, "that is just like the old soldiers of the Empire, who for twenty years after Napoleon's death stoutly maintained that he was still alive."

Since passing across the Upper Ganges, fifteen days previous to this, a fertile country had opened before us, called the Doâb, a district lying in the angle formed by the Ganges and the Jumna, which two rivers unite near Allahabad.

My impressions of the Doâb are of alluvial plains

cleared by the Brahmins twenty centuries before the
Christian era, farming operations of the rudest description
carried on by the peasantry, vast canal works due to
English engineers, fields of the cotton plant, which especially thrives in this part of the country, the groans of
the cotton-mill machinery at work near every village,
mingled with the songs of the men who are employed
about it.

We went on our way very comfortably. Scenery and
situations changed before our eyes, while we enjoyed in
luxury the climax of the art of locomotion.

What mode of progression could be superior to this?

We reached the left bank of the Jumna. This important stream forms the boundary of Rajasthan, the
country of the Rajahs, dividing it from Hindostan, or the
country of the Hindoos.

We found that an early flood had already raised the
waters of the Jumna. The current was rapid, but
although this made our transit somewhat less easy, it
did not hinder it at all. Banks took some few precautions, found a suitable landing-place, and within half
an hour Steam House was mounting the opposite bank
of the river.

Railway trains require massive bridges to be built at
great expense; one of these, of tubular construction,
spans the Jumna at the fortress of Pelimghur near
Delhi. But our Behemoth drew his double cars over the
surface of the current with as much ease as along the best
macadamized high-road.

Beyond the Jumna lay several of the towns which our
engineer intended to pass by unvisited.

Among these was Gwalior, situated near the river
Sawunrika, built on a basaltic rock, with its superb
mosque of Musjid, its palace of Pâl, its curious Gate of
the Elephants, it famous fortress, and the Vihura erected
by Buddhists. The modern town of Lashkar, built at a
little distance, forms a singular contrast to this ancient
city, and competes in trade with it vigorously.

It was at Gwalior that the Ranee of Jansi, the devoted friend of Nana Sahib, defended herself heroically to the last. There, as we have already said, she fell by the hand of Colonel Munro, during an engagement with two squadrons of the British troops, where he was in command of a battalion of his regiment, and from that moment dated the mortal hatred borne towards him by the Nabob, who sought till death to gratify it by revenge.

Yes! it certainly was desirable that Sir Edward Munro should not renew his recollections of the scenes which took place before the gates of Gwalior !

After Gwalior we passed Antri, and its vast plain broken by numerous peaks, like islands in an archipelago.

Then Duttiah, which has not been in existence for more than five centuries. It possesses a central fortress, elegant houses, temples of various forms, the deserted palace of Birsing-Deo, and the arsenal of Tope-Kana, the whole forming the capital of the province of Duttiah, which lies in the northern angle of Bundelkund, and is under British protection. Antri and Duttiah, as well as Gwalior, were seriously compromised by the insurrectional disturbances of 1857.

On the 22nd of September Jansi was passed at a considerable distance. This city is the most important military station in the Bundelkund, and the spirit of revolt is strong in the lower classes of its population. The town is comparatively modern, and has a great trade in Indian muslins, and blue cotton cloths. There are no ancient remains in this place, but it is interesting to visit its citadel, whose walls the English artillery and projectiles failed to destroy, also the Necropolis of the rajahs, which is remarkably picturesque.

This was the chief stronghold of the sepoy mutineers in Central India. There the intrepid Ranee instigated the first rising, which speedily spread throughout the Bundelkund.

There Sir Hugh Rose maintained an engagement

which lasted no less than six days, during which time he lost fifteen per cent. of his force.

There, in spite of the obstinate resistance of a garrison of twelve thousand sepoys, and backed by an army of twenty thousand, Tantia Topi, Balao Rao (brother of the Nana), and last, not least, the Rance herself, were compelled to yield to the superiority of British arms.

It was there, at Jansi, that Colonel Munro had saved the life of his sergeant, McNeil, and given up to him his last drop of water. Yes! Jansi of all places must be avoided in a journey where the route was planned and marked out by Sir Edward's warmest friends!

After passing Jansi, we were detained for several hours by an encounter with travellers of whom Kâlagani had previously spoken.

It was about eleven o'clock. Breakfast was over, and we were lounging under the verandah, or in the saloon, while Behemoth plodded steadily on at a moderate speed. The road was magnificent. Shaded by lofty trees it passed through fields of cotton and grain. The weather was fine, the sun very hot. All we could wish for was a metropolitan water-cart, to keep down the puffs of fine white dust which occasionally rose round our equipage.

But after a while the atmosphere appeared to become absolutely darkened with clouds of dust as dense as any ever blown up by the simoom of the Libyan Desert.

"I cannot imagine the cause of such a phenomenon," said Banks, "for the wind blows quite a light breeze."

"Probably Kâlagani can explain it," said Colonel Munro.

He was called, and, entering the verandah, looked along the road, and at once said,—

"It is a long caravan going northward, and is most likely a party of the Brinjarees I spoke of to you, Mr. Banks."

"Ah! and no doubt you will find some old friends among them."

" Possibly, sahib ; I lived a long time among those wandering tribes."

" Perhaps you will want to leave us and join them again," remarked Captain Hood.

" Not at all," answered Kâlagani.

Half an hour later it was proved that his opinion was correct. A moving wall of oxen advanced, and our mighty elephant himself was brought to a standstill. There was nothing to regret in this enforced halt, however, for a most curious spectacle was presented to our observations.

A drove of four or five thousand oxen encumbered the road, and, as our guide had supposed, they belonged to a caravan of Brinjarees.

" These people," said Banks, " are the Zingaris of Hindostan. They are a people rather than a tribe, and have no fixed abode, dwelling under tents in summer, in huts during the winter or rainy season. They are the porters and carriers of India, and I saw how they worked during the insurrection of 1857. By a sort of tacit agreement between the belligerents, their convoys were permitted to pass through the disturbed provinces. In fact, they kept up the supply of provisions to both armies. If these Brinjarees belong to one part of India more than to another, I should say it was Rajpootana, and perhaps more particularly the kingdom of Milwar. Pray examine them attentively, my dear Maucler, as they pass before you in defile."

Our equipage was prudently drawn up on one side of the great highway. Nothing could have withstood this avalanche of horned cattle, even wild beasts hasten out of their way.

Following Bank's advice, I set myself to observe closely the enormous procession as it passed by, and the first thing I noticed was that our Steam Elephant, so accustomed to create surprise and admiration, seemed scarcely to attract the attention of these people at all ; they looked as if nothing ever could astonish them.

Both men and women of the race were extremely handsome ; the former tall and strong, with fine features, curly hair, and a clear bronze complexion ; they wore long tunics and turbans, and carried lances, bucklers, or round shields, and large swords slung across their shoulders. The latter, also very tall and well formed, were dressed in becoming bodices with full skirts, a loose mantle enveloping the whole form in graceful drapery. They wore jewels in their ears, and necklaces, bracelets, bangles, and anklets, made of gold, ivory, or shells. Thousands of oxen paced quietly along with these men, women, old men, and children. They had neither harness nor halter, only bells or red tassels on their heads, and double packs thrown across their backs, which contained wheat and other grains.

A whole tribe journeyed in this manner, under the directions of an elected chief, called the "naik," whose power is despotic while it lasts. He controls the movements of the caravan, fixes the hours for the start and the halt, and arranges the dispositions of the camp.

I was struck by the magnificent appearance of a large bull, who with superb and imperial step led the van. He was covered with a bright-coloured cloth, ornamented with bells and shell embroidery, and I asked Banks if he knew what was the special office of this splendid animal.

"Kâlagani will of course be able to tell us," answered he. "Where is the fellow?"

He was called, but did not make his appearance, and search being made, it was found he had left Steam House.

"No doubt he has gone to renew acquaintance with some old comrade," said Colonel Munro. "He will return before we resume our journey."

This seemed very natural. There was nothing in the temporary absence of the man to occasion uneasiness, but somehow it haunted me uncomfortably.

"Well," said Banks, "to the best of my belief this bull represents, or is an emblem of, their deity. Where he goes, they follow ; where he stops, there they encamp ; but of course we are to suppose he is in reality under the secret control of the 'naik.' Anyhow, he is to these wanderers an embodiment of their religion."

The *cortège* seemed interminable, and for two hours there was no sign of an approaching end. Soon afterwards, however, the rearguard came in sight, and at last I perceived Kâlagani accompanied by a native who was not of the Brinjaree type. They were conversing together very coolly, and he was no doubt one who, as Kâlagani had frequently done, had joined the caravan for a time only. Probably they were talking of the country which the caravan had just passed through, and across which lay the route by which our new guide had undertaken to lead us.

This man, who was the last of all the procession to pass us, paused for a moment before Steam House.

He looked at the equipage with some interest, and I thought his eye rested particularly on Sir Edward Munro ; but without uttering a word he made a parting sign to Kâlagani, rejoined the troop, and disappeared in a cloud of dust.

Kâlagani then came up, and before any questions were asked addressed himself to Colonel Munro and simply saying,—

"One of my old comrades, who has been with the caravan for the last two months," he resumed his place in our train, and we were speedily moving along a road now deeply marked by the footprints of thousands of men and oxen.

Next day, the 24th of September, we halted to pass the night a little to the east of Ourtcha on the left bank of the Bettwa, which is one of the chief tributaries of the Jumna. There is nothing to see or say about Ourtcha. It is the old capital of Bundelkund, and was a flourishing town during the earlier part of the seventeenth century. But hard blows from the Mahrattas on one side, and the Mongols on the other, reduced it to a low condition

G

from which it has never recovered ; so that, at the present
time, one of the great cities of Central India is nothing
more than a large village, miserably housing a few
hundred peasants.

I said we encamped on the banks of the Bettwa, but
the halt was made at some distance from the river,
which, we learned, had considerably overflowed its
banks. Night was coming on, and it would be necessary
next day to examine carefully the nature of the ground
before attempting a passage. We therefore spent our
evening in the usual way, and retired to rest.

Except under very peculiar circumstances, we never
kept watch by night. There seemed to be no occasion
for it. Could anybody run away with our houses ? No !
Could they steal our elephant ? Rather not ! Nothing
was more unlikely than an attack of thieves ; but at all
times our two dogs, Fan and Niger, were on the alert,
and ready to give notice of approaching footsteps.

This very thing happened that night. Their violent
barking aroused us about two in the morning.

When I opened the door of my room, I found all my
companions on foot.

"Is anything the matter ?" inquired Colonel Munro.

"The dogs seem to think so," replied Banks. "I
don't believe they would bark like that for nothing."

"I should not wonder if a panther had coughed in the
jungle," said Hood. "Let's take our guns and make a
search."

McNeil, Kâlagani, and Goûmi were all out listening
and trying to find out what was going on. We joined them.

"Well," said the captain, "I suppose a few wild animals
have passed on their way to the drinking-place ?"

"Kâlagani thinks this is something very different,"
replied Sergeant McNeil.

"What then, Kâlagani ?"

"I don't know yet, colonel," said the Indian ; "but certainly neither panthers, tigers, nor jackals. I fancy I
can discern a confused mass among the trees—"

"Let's have at them at once!" exclaimed the captain, with eager hopes of his fiftieth tiger.

"Wait, Hood, wait," said Banks ; "caution is desirable in this case."

"But we are in force, and well armed! I want to be at the bottom of this disturbance," persisted the captain.

"All right then," cried Banks. "Munro, you must remain in camp with McNeil and the other men, while Hood, Maucler, Kâlagani and I go to reconnoitre."

All this time the dogs continued to bark, but without any symptoms of the fury which they always displayed on the approach of wild beasts.

"Come along, Fox!" cried Captain Hood, beckoning to his servant.

Fan and Niger darted into the thicket. We followed them, and presently distinguished the sound of footsteps. It seemed as though the scouts of a large party were prowling round our camp. A few figures vanished silently among the bushes.

The two dogs, barking loudly, ran backwards and forwards some paces in advance of us.

"Who goes there?" shouted Captain Hood.

No answer.

"These people either do not choose to speak or else understand no English," said Banks.

"Well—give it them in Hindoostance! Tell them we will fire if they don't answer."

In the dialect of Central India Kâlagani summoned the invisible rovers to advance and show themselves.

Still no answer.

A rifle-shot broke the silence. The impetuous captain could stand it no longer, and had taken-aim apparently at a shadow flitting through the trees.

The report was followed by a confused rushing sound, as if a multitude of people were dispersing right and left. Fan and Niger ran forwards, and then, returning to us quietly, showed no further uneasiness.

"Well, they beat a retreat double quick, these fellows, whoever they were," exclaimed Hood.

"That is very certain," returned Banks; "and now, whether they were robbers or rovers, all we have to do is to get back to Steam House. But we must set a watch till daybreak."

In a very few minutes we had rejoined our party. McNeil, Goûmi, and Fox arranged to take turns as sentries, and we once more retired to our cabins.

The night passed without disturbance; it was clear that, seeing we were on our guard, the visitors had decamped.

Next day, the 25th of September, while preparation was being made for a start, Colonel Munro, Hood, McNeil, Kâlagani and I set out to explore the borders of the forest. We saw no trace whatever of the nocturnal adventurers, and on our return found Banks busily arranging for the passage of the river Bettwa, whose tawny waters were flowing far beyond their accustomed bed. The current was running at so rapid a rate, that Behemoth would have to make head against it, to avoid being carried down stream.

The engineer, field-glass in hand, was endeavouring to determine our landing-place on the opposite bank.

The Bettwa was at this point about a mile in width. Our train had as yet crossed no river so broad.

"What," said I, "becomes of travellers and traders when they are stopped by floods like this? These currents resemble rapids; ordinary ferry-boats could not resist them."

"Why! it is quite simple," replied Captain Hood; "they stay where they are."

"They can always cross if they have elephants," said Banks.

"You don't mean to say elephants can swim such distances?"

"Of course they can, and the thing is managed thus,"

answered the engineer. " All the baggage is placed on the backs of these—"

"Proboscidians," suggested Hood, recollecting his friend the Dutchman's fine words.

"And the mahouts force them, at first reluctantly, to enter the stream. The animals hesitate, draw back, trumpet loudly ; but finally make up their minds to face the difficulty, and, beginning to swim, gallantly effect the passage. It must be admitted that some are occasionally swept away by the current and drowned, but that rarely happens if any experienced person is in charge."

" Well," said Hood, " Behemoth is thoroughly amphibious, and no doubt will make a fine passage."

We all took our places ; Kâlouth by his furnace, Storr in the howdah, Banks acting as steersman. With gentle pace the elephant began his march. His great feet were covered, but the water was for about fifty feet too shallow to float him. Great caution was requisite, and the train moved slowly from *terra firma*.

All of a sudden we became aware that the sounds we had heard in the night were renewed and drawing near us. About a hundred creatures, gesticulating and grimacing, issued from the woods.

" Monkeys, by Jove ! " exclaimed Hood, with a burst of laughter, as a whole regiment of apes advanced in close order towards Steam House.

"What on earth do they want ? " inquired McNeil.

" Of course they are going to attack us," answered the belligerent captain.

" No, you have nothing to fear," said Kâlagani, who was watching them.

" Well, but what are they up to ? " repeated McNeil.

" They only want to cross the river with us," said the Indian.

And Kâlagani was right. These were not insolent gibbons, with long hairy arms and importunate manners, nor were they members of the aristocratic family which inhabits the palace at Benares ; but black monkeys, the largest in India, very active, and with white whiskers round their smooth faces, which make them look like old lawyers. In fantastic airs and attitudes they almost rivalled our friend Mathias van Guitt himself.

I then learnt that these apes are sacred throughout India. One legend asserts that they are the descendants of Rama, who conquered the island of Ceylon.

At Amber they occupy the Zenana palace, and do the honours to visitors. It is expressly forbidden to kill them; several English officers have lost their lives through disregard of this law.

These monkeys are usually very gentle, and easily domesticated, but are dangerous if attacked, and when only slightly wounded become, according to the statement of M. Louis Rousselet, quite as formidable as hyenas or panthers. But we had no intention of attacking them, and Captain Hood's gun was not called into requisition. Could Kâlagani be right in saying that these creatures, unable otherwise to cross the river, intended to avail themselves of our floating equipage?

We were speedily to see that it was so.

When, after passing through the shallows, Behemoth reached the bed of the river, our train floated after him, and, encountering a kind of eddy from a turn in the bank, remained at first almost stationary.

Just then the troop of monkeys approached, wading and dabbling in the shallow water. They made no demonstration of hostility; but suddenly the whole party, males, females, old and young, began to gambol and spring towards us, and finally seizing each other by the hand they fairly bounded up on our train, which actually seemed to be waiting for them.

In a few seconds there were a dozen on Behemoth's back, thirty on the top of each carriage, and soon we had quite a hundred passengers, gay, familiar, even talkative (at least among themselves, no doubt congratulating one another on the fortunate chance by which they had secured their passage across the river.

Behemoth now fairly entered the current, and, boldly facing it, proceeded on his way.

For an instant Banks looked anxiously at the apes, but they disposed themselves judiciously, so as to trim the flotilla. They sat or clung in all directions over the back of the elephant, on his neck, on his tusks, even on his upraised trunk, caring nothing for the jets of steam which it cast forth.

They clustered on the arched roofs of our carriages, some squatting down, some standing upright, some on all fours, others dangling by the tail from the verandah roofs. Steam House maintained its equilibrium, and the excess of cargo proved to be quite immaterial.

Captain Hood was immensely amused, and his man Fox excessively astonished. He soon made friends with the free and easy creatures, who were grimacing on all sides of him, and began to do the honours of the house. He talked to them, shook hands, made his best bows, offered lumps of sugar, and would willingly have handed sweetmeats all round if Monsieur Parazard would have allowed it.

Behemoth worked his four feet strenuously; they beat the water, and acted like paddles.

Drifting downwards in the current, he followed the direction which took us towards the landing-place. This we safely reached in about half an hour; and the moment our train touched the shore, the whole troop of monkeys sprang down, and with numberless absurd antics and capers scampered off as hard as they could go.

"They might as well have said 'Thank'ee'!" cried Fox, quite disgusted with the bad manners of his fellow-passengers.

CHAPTER VIII.

HOOD VERSUS BANKS.

HAVING passed the Bettwa, we found ourselves already sixty-two miles from the station of Etawah, where we had left the Dutchman, Van Guitt.

Four days passed without incident—without even any sport for Captain Hood, wild animals being scarce in that part of Scind.

"Upon my word," he kept repeating in tones of great annoyance, "I begin to fear I shall arrive at Bombay without having bagged my fiftieth!"

Kâlagani evidently knew this thinly-peopled region perfectly, and guided us across it most admirably. On the 29th September our train began to ascend the northern slope of the Vindhyas, in order to reach the pass of Sirgour.

Hitherto we had met with no obstacle or difficulty, although this country is one of the worst in repute of all India, because it is a favourite retreat of criminals. Robbers haunt the highways, and it is here that the Dacoits carry on their double trade of thieves and poisoners. Great caution is desirable when travelling in this district.

Steam House was now about to penetrate the very worst part of the Bundelkund, namely, the mountainous region of the Vindhyas.

We were within about sixty miles of Jubbulpore, the nearest station on the railway between Bombay and Allahabad; it was no great distance, but we could not expect to get over the ground as quickly as we had done on the plains of Scind. Steep ascents, bad roads, rocky ground, sharp turnings, and narrow defiles,—all these must be looked for, and would reduce the rate of our speed. It would be necessary to reconnoitre carefully our line of march, as well as the halting-places, and during both day and night keep a very sharp look-out. Kâlagani was the first to urge these precautions. It was certainly wise to be prepared for every contingency ; prudence is always a virtue.

Nevertheless, we had little to fear, being a numerous party, thoroughly armed, and, as it were, garrisoning two strong houses and a castle, which it was hardly likely marauders of any sort, Dacoits or even Thugs, supposing any still lurked in this wild part of the Bundelkund, would venture to assault.

The pass of Sirgour was attained with no great difficulty. In some places it was necessary to put on steam, when Behemoth instantly displayed power amply sufficient for the occasion.

Kâlagani appeared so well acquainted with the winding passes among which we found ourselves, that we ceased to feel anxiety as to the route we were on. He never showed the smallest hesitation, but led the way confidently among deep gorges, lofty precipices, and dense forests of pines and other alpine trees, even where cross-roads would have puzzled many guides.

At times he stopped the train, and went forward to survey the road, but it was to ascertain its condition, which after the rainy season was often torn up by torrents, and, retreat being difficult, it was awkward to come upon such chasms unawares.

The weather was perfect. The rains were over, and the burning sky was veiled by light mists, which tempered the solar rays, so that the heat we experienced was temperate, very endurable for travellers so well sheltered as we were. It was easy for our sportsmen to shoot what game we needed for the table without going any great distance from Steam House.

Captain Hood, however, and doubtless Fox also,

regretted the absence of the wild beasts which abounded in the Terrai. But how could they hope to find lions, tigers, and panthers, where there was nothing for them to eat?

If, however, there was a lack of carnivora, we found occasion to make better acquaintance with Indian elephants—I mean wild elephants, of whom hitherto we had seen but rare examples.

It was about noon on the 30th September that we perceived a pair of these superb animals in front of our train. On our approach, they left the road to let us pass, as though alarmed by the novel appearance of our equipage.

Even Captain Hood never thought of firing at the magnificent creatures unnecessarily. We all stood admiring them thus roaming at liberty their native wilds, where streams, torrents, and pastures afforded all they required.

"What a fine opportunity now for our friend Van Guitt to deliver a lecture on zoology!" cried the captain.

Everybody knows that India is, *par excellence*, the country for elephants; the species is rather smaller than the African elephant; it abounds in the various provinces of the peninsula, and is sought after also in Burmah, Siam, in the territories east of the Bay of Bengal.

They are usually captured by means of a "keddah," which is an enclosure surrounded by palisades. Sometimes it is intended to secure a whole herd at once, and then the hunters assemble to the number of three or four hundred, under command of a "jemidar," that is, a native sergeant, or headman, and drive them gradually towards the "keddah."

This they are enticed to enter by the aid of tame elephants trained to the business; they are then separated, and have their hind legs shackled. The capture is then complete. But this method, besides being tedious and troublesome, is generally unsuccessful with the large male elephants, who are bolder, and cunning enough to burst through the circle of beaters, thus escaping imprisonment in the keddah. The tame female elephants are appointed to follow these males for several days, the mahouts, wrapped in dark clothes remain on their backs, and at last the unsuspecting elephants, when peacefully slumbering, are seized, chained, and led away captive before they recover from their first surprise.

In former times, as I have already had occasion to mention, elephants were taken in deep pits dug near their haunts, but by falling into these, which were about fifteen feet deep ; the animals were often hurt or even killed, and the barbarous practice is now almost given up.

In Bengal and Nepaul, where the lasso is still in use, the chase becomes highly exciting and replete with adventure. Well-trained elephants are mounted by three men ; one, the mahout, rides on the neck, and directs the animal's movements ; another behind, whose duty it is to spur and goad him. while the hunter is seated on his back, armed with a lasso, the noose ready prepared to fling. Thus equipped, the pursuit may last for hours, over plains and through forests, the hunters running great danger in the chase, but at length the huge quarry is lassoed, falls heavily, and is at the mercy of his captors.

By these different methods a vast number of elephants is annually caught in India. It is not a bad speculation. The price of a female elephant is sometimes 280*l.*, of a male 800*l.*, or even 2000*l.*, if he is of noble race.

But are the animals which cost such sums really so useful as to be worth it ?

Yes, provided they are well fed. They must have six or seven hundred pounds' weight of green fodder in every eighteen hours, that is about the amount allowed for average rations, and are then fit for active service ; for the transport of troops and military stores, transport of artillery and waggons in mountainous countries, or through jungle impassable for horses ; also in many great works of civil engineering, and other undertakings, where they are employed as beasts of burden.

These strong and docile giants are easily and quickly trained, seeming by instinct to be disposed to obedience ; they are universally employed in Hindostan, and as they do not multiply in captivity, it is necessary to keep up the supply for the country and for exportation by continually hunting those which roam the forests. Not-withstanding this the herds of wild elephants appear in no way diminished. Numbers are still to be found in the different kingdoms of India.

Indeed, as far as we were concerned, far too many were at liberty, and this I shall presently show.

The two elephants in advance of us drew aside as I described, so as to allow our train to pass by them, im-mediately afterwards resuming their march in the rear.

Presently several other elephants came in sight, and, quickening their pace, overtook and joined the pair we had just passed. In a quarter of an hour as many as a dozen were behind us. They were evidently watching our equipage, and followed us at a distance of fifty yards. They did not try to overtake us, still less did they show any intention of leaving our company. They might easily have done so, for an elephant's pace can be much more rapid than at first sight one would suppose, and among the rugged steeps of the Vindhyas Behemoth could travel but slowly. But their object evidently was to assemble in greater numbers. As they advanced they uttered peremptory calls, which appeared to be a summons to companions lingering behind, for cries, unmistakably in answer, sounded in the distance.

By one o'clock a troop of full thirty elephants followed us closely, and it was quite likely the number would increase.

Herds of these animals, consisting of thirty individuals, and forming a family party more or less nearly related, are frequently seen together ; at times a formidable assemblage of at least a hundred are encountered with no great pleasure by travellers.

We all stood in the verandah behind our second carriage, and watched proceedings with some anxiety.

"The numbers continue to increase," remarked Banks. "I suppose they mean to bring all the elephants in the district about us?"

"But," said I, "they cannot call to each other at any great distance."

"No," replied the engineer; "but they have a very acute sense of smell, and we know it, because tame elephants detect the presence of wild ones three or four miles off."

"Why, it is like a migration—an exodus!" said Colonel Munro. "We ought to increase our speed, Banks."

"Behemoth is doing his best, Munro. He has heavy work on this steep and rugged way."

"What's the use of hurrying?" cried Hood, always delighted with fresh adventure. "Let them come along with us, the jolly beasts! They form an escort just suited to us! The country, which seemed so desolate and deserted, is much more interesting now, and we go along with a retinue fit for a rajah!"

"We shall have to submit to their presence certainly," said Banks. "I don't see how we are to prevent it."

"Why, what in the world are you afraid of?" asked the captain. "You know very well that a herd is always less dangerous than a solitary elephant. These are good, quiet beasts! Sheep, big sheep, with trunks —that's all!"

"Hood's enthusiasm is rising fast," said Colonel Munro. "I am willing to believe that if these animals remain in the rear and keep their distance, we have nothing to fear; but if they take it into their heads to try to pass us on this narrow road, the consequences might be serious!"

"Besides," I added, "what sort of reception will they

give Behemoth, if they find themselves face to face with him ? "

" Oh, nonsense ! They will only salute him ! " cried Hood. " They will make grand salaams to him, as Prince Gourou Singh's elephants did ! "

" But those were tame elephants, sir, and well trained," remarked Sergeant McNeil very sensibly.

" Well, those fellows behind there will become tame too. Their astonishment at meeting our giant will produce the deepest respect."

Our friend's admiration for the artificial elephant continued unabated ; that *chef-d'œuvre* of mechanism, created by the hand of an English engineer.

" Besides," he continued, " these animals are intelligent ; they reason, compare, and judge. They can associate ideas like human beings."

" I question that," said Banks.

" Question that, do you ? " cried the captain. " One would almost think you had never lived in India ! Are not these excellent fellows put to all manner of domestic service ? Have we any servant to equal them ? Is not the elephant always ready to be useful? Don't you know, Maucler, what accounts of him are given by the best informed authors ? According to them, the elephant is devoted to those he loves, carries their parcels, gathers flowers for them, goes out to shop in the bazaars, buys his own sugar-cane, bananas, and mangoes, and pays for them himself, guards the house from wild beasts, and takes the children out walking more carefully than the best nurse in all England. He is kind, grateful, has a prodigious memory, and never forgets either a benefit or an injury. And then so tender-hearted ! Why, an elephant won't hurt a fly, if he can help it ! Look here ! a friend of mine told me this himself. He saw a lady-bird placed on a big stone, and the elephant was ordered to crush the little insect. Not a bit of it ! The good beast would not put his foot on the creature ; neither commands nor blows could drive him to the cruel deed !

But directly he was told to lift it, he picked it up most tenderly with the delicate tip of his trunk, and let it fly away! Now then, Banks, I hope you will admit that the elephant is good and generous, superior to every other animal in creation, even to the ape and the dog. Are not the natives in the right when they attribute to him almost human intelligence?"

And the captain wound up his tirade by taking off his hat, and making a flourishing bow to the formidable army, which, with measured pace, came marching after us.

"Well spoken, Hood!" exclaimed Colonel Munro, with a smile. "Elephants have in you a very warm advocate."

"Don't you think I am in the right, colonel?"

"Hood may possibly be right," said Banks; "but I am disposed to agree with the opinion of Sanderson, a great hunter, and the best authority in such matters."

"Well; and what may this Sanderson say?" cried the captain in a tone of contempt.

"He maintains that the elephant possesses no unusual amount of intelligence, and that his most wonderful performances are simply the result of absolute obedience to orders given more or less secretly by their drivers."

"Oh! indeed!" exclaimed Hood with some warmth.

"And he points to the fact," continued Banks, "that the Hindoos have never chosen the elephant to symbolize wisdom; but in their sculptures and sacred carvings have given in this respect the preference to the fox, the crow, and the ape."

"Oh! oh! I protest!" cried the captain vehemently.

"Protest as much as you like, but listen to me. Sanderson adds that in the elephant the organ of obedience is phrenologically developed to an extraordinary degree—any one may see the protuberance on his skull. Besides, he lets himself be taken in traps which are perfectly childish in their simplicity, such as holes covered over with sticks and branches, from which he never contrives to escape. He is easily decoyed into enclosures which no other wild animal would go near. And if he escapes from captivity, he is retaken with a facility which is very little credit to his good sense. Even experience does not teach him prudence."

"Poor beggars!" interposed Hood in a comic tone, "what a character this engineer is giving you, to be sure!"

"I will add, as my final argument," continued Banks, "that it is often extremely difficult to domesticate and train these creatures, especially while they are young, and when they belong to the weaker sex."

"Why, that only proves more than ever that they resemble human beings!" exclaimed Hood joyfully. "Isn't it much easier to manage men than children and women?"

"My dear fellow, I do not see that either you or I, as bachelors, can be competent to decide such a question as that."

"Ha! ha! well answered!"

"In short," added Banks, "I do not think we ought to place too much reliance on the amiability of the elephant; if anything were to excite a troop of them to fury, it would be impossible to resist them, and as for those who are at this moment escorting us to the south, I heartily wish that they had urgent business in the opposite direction!"

"While you and Hood have been disputing about them, my dear Banks, their number has increased to an alarming extent," remarked Colonel Munro.

CHAPTER IX.

A HUNDRED AGAINST ONE.

SIR EDWARD was not mistaken. A herd of from fifty to sixty elephants was now behind our train. They advanced in close ranks and were already so near to Steam House—within ten yards—that it was possible to survey them minutely.

At their head marched one of the largest in the herd, although its height, measured from the shoulder, was certainly not more than nine feet. As I remarked before, the Asiatic elephant is smaller than the African, which is frequently twelve feet high, and its tusks are in proportion. In the island of Ceylon a certain number of animals are found deprived of these appendages, but "mucknas," which is the name given them, are rare on the mainland of India.

Behind the first elephant came several females, who in general are the leaders, while the males remain in the rear. Apparently on this occasion the usual order was changed, because of our presence on the line of march. The males in fact have nothing to do with the guidance of the herd. They have not the charge of their young ones ; they cannot know when the babies ought to have a rest, nor can they tell what sort of camping-place is most fit for them. It is the females who, figuratively, "carry the tusks" of the household and direct the great migrations.

It was really difficult to answer the question of why they were now on the move, whether it was to seek more abundant pasture, or to escape the sting of certain venomous insects, or a mere fancy to follow our strange

H

equipage ; the country was open enough, and according to their usual custom, when they are not in wooded regions, these elephants journey by daylight. Before long we should see whether they would stop at nightfall, as we should ourselves be obliged to do.

"Hood," said I, "see how our rearguard has increased! Do you still persist in thinking there is no danger?"

"Pooh!" said the captain. "Why should those animals want to do us any harm? They are not like tigers, are they, Fox?"

"Nor even panthers!" was the answer of the servant, who always chimed in with his master's ideas.

But at this reply I perceived Kâlagani shake his head disapprovingly. He evidently did not share in the perfect equanimity of the two hunters.

"You seem to be uneasy, Kâlagani," said Banks, looking at him.

"Cannot the speed of the train be increased?" was the man's only reply.

"It will be rather difficult," returned the engineer, "but we will try."

So saying, Banks left the verandah, and ascended to the howdah, in which Storr was standing. Almost immediately the snorts of Behemoth increased, as well as the speed of the train.

Very little, though, for the road was rough. But even if our rate had been redoubl d, the state of things would have remained the same. The herd of elephants also advanced more rapidly, and the distance between them and Steam House did not diminish.

Several hours passed thus without any important alteration taking place. After dinner we resumed our places on the verandah of the second carriage.

The road now stretched away behind us for two miles or so in a straight line. Our view of it was no longer intercepted by sudden turnings.

To our extreme uneasiness we perceived that the

number of elephants had increased within the last hour !
We now counted at least a hundred.

The creatures marched in double or treble file, according to the width of the road, silently, at an even step,
with their trunks in the air.   It was like the advance of
the tide flowing quietly in.   All was calm now, to continue the metaphor, but if a tempest lashed into fury
this moving mass, to what danger might we not be
exposed ?

In the meantime evening came on.   There would be
no moon, nor would the stars give any light, for a sort
of fog or haze shrouded the heavens.

As Banks said, it would be impossible to follow such
a difficult road in the dark.   He resolved, therefore, to
halt as soon as the valley widened, or we met with some
gorge into which we could go, and allow the alarming-
looking herd to pass us, and continue their migration
to the south.

But would they do so ?   Might they not halt in or
near our encampment ?

This was the great question.

With nightfall came a sort of agitation among the
elephants, which we had not observed during the day.
A sort of roar, powerful but dull, escaped from their
mighty lungs.   To this uproar succeeded another
peculiar noise.

" What does that mean ? " asked the colonel.

" That is the sound they make," replied Kâlagani,
" when they are in presence of an enemy "

" And it is we, it can only be we, whom they consider
as such," said Banks.

" I fear so," replied the native.

The sound now resembled distant thunder.   It
recalled that which is produced in the side-scenes of a
theatre by the vibration of sheets of iron.   Rubbing
the extremity of their trunks on the ground, the
elephants sent forth prolonged breaths with a deep and
sullen roar.

It was now nine in the evening.

We had reached a sort of little plain, almost circular, and half a mile in width, from which debouched the road to the lake Pu·uria, near which Kâlagani had proposed our halting. But this lake being still ten miles off, it was hopeless to think of reaching it that night.

Banks now gave the signal to stop. Behemoth became stationary, but he was not unharnessed. The fires were not even raked out. Storr received orders to keep up the pressure, so that the train might move on again at a moment's notice. We were thus ready for any emergency.

Colonel Munro retired to his room. Banks and Hood did not care to go to bed, and I preferred sitting up with them. All our servants were also afoot. But what could we possibly do, if the elephants took it into their heads to attack Steam House?

For the first hour a dull murmur continued around our encampment. The herd was evidently spreading over the little plain. Were they merely crossing it, and pursuing their way southwards?

"That's possible, after all," said Banks.

"It is even more than probable," added Captain Hood, whose optimism was never at fault.

Towards eleven o'clock the sounds began to diminish, and at ten minutes past they had totally ceased.

It was a perfectly calm night, so that the slightest noise would have reached our ears. Nothing was to be heard but the panting of Behemoth, and nothing was to be seen but the sparks which flew occasionally from his trunk.

"Well!" remarked Hood, "wasn't I right? Those fine fellows have taken their departure."

"And a pleasant journey to them," I rejoined.

"I am not at all sure they are gone," said Banks, shaking his head. "But we must find out."

Then calling to the engine-driver,—

"Storr," he said "the signal-lamps."

" Ay, ay, sir ! "

In twenty seconds' time the two electric lights blazed from Behemoth's eyes, and by automatic mechanism were directed in turn to every point of the horizon.

There lay the elephants in a great circle round Steam House, motionless, perhaps asleep. The brilliant light turned upon their dark bodies seemed to animate them with supernatural life. By a natural optical illusion the monsters assumed gigantic proportions, rivalling our Behemoth. Aroused by the glare they started, as if touched by a fiery sting. Trunks were raised, and tusks pointed, as if the creatures were making ready for a rush at the train. Roars issued from each vast throat. This sudden fury communicated itself to all, and round our encampment soon arose a deafening concert, as if a hundred clarions at once were sounding a startling call.

" Out with the light ! " called Banks.

The electric current was suddenly interrupted, and as suddenly the commotion ceased.

" They are there, you see, camped in a circle," said the engineer ; "and there they will still be at day break."

" Hum ! " observed Captain Hood, whose confidence appeared to be somewhat shaken.

What was to be done next ? Kâlagani was consulted. He did not attempt to conceal the anxiety he felt.

Could we leave the encampment under cover of the darkness ? That was impossible. Besides, what use would it be ? The herd of elephants would certainly follow us, and the difficulties of the road would be far greater than by day.

It was therefore agreed that the departure should not be attempted until dawn. We would then proceed with all possible prudence and celerity, but without startling or offending our formidable retinue.

" And suppose these animals persist in escorting us ? " asked.

" We will endeavour to reach some spot where Steam

House can be put out of their reach," answered Banks.

" Shall we find such a spot before we get beyond the Vindhyas ? " asked the captain.

" There is one," said the Hindoo.

" What is it ? " demanded Banks.

" Lake Puturia."

" At what distance is it ? "

" About nine miles."

" But elephants swim," replied Banks, "perhaps better than any other quadruped. They have been seen to keep themselves on the surface of the water for more than half a day ! Now, is it not to be feared that they might follow us into Lake Puturia, and thus the situation of Steam House be made still more serious ? "

" I cannot see any other way of escaping their attack ! " said the native.

" Then we will try it ! " said the engineer.

It was indeed the only thing to be done. The elephants might perhaps not venture to swim after us, and, if they did, we might outstrip them.

We waited impatiently for day, which was not long in appearing. No hostile demonstration was made during the night, but at sunrise not an elephant had stirred, and Steam House was surrounded on all sides.

All at once a general move was made, as if the creatures were obeying a word of command. They shook their trunks, rubbed their tusks on the ground, made their toilet by squirting water all over their bodies, gathered several mouthfuls of the thick grass with which the ground was covered, and finally approached so near to Steam House that we could have touched them through the windows.

Banks, however, expressly forbade us to provoke them It was important that no pretext should be given for a sudden attack.

In the meantime several elephants pressed up close to Behemoth. They evidently wished to ascertain what the enormous animal, now standing so motionless, could be. Did they consider him as a relation? Did they suspect that he was endowed with marvellous power?

On the day before they had had no opportunity for seeing him at work, for their first ranks had always kept a certain distance from the rear of the train.

But what would they do when they heard him snort and bellow, when his trunk ejected torrents of vapour, when they saw him raise and set down his great feet and begin to march, dragging the two great vans after him?

Colonel Munro, Captain Hood, Kâlagani, and I took our places in the fore part of the train. Sergeant McNeil and his companions were at the back.

Kâlouth, at the furnaces, kept up the supply of fuel, so that the pressure of vapour had already reached five atmospheres.

Banks was in the howdah with Storr, and kept his hand on the regulator.

The moment for departure came. At a sign from Banks, the driver touched the spring, and an ear-piercing whistle resounded through the air.

The elephants raised their heads, then, drawing back a little, they left the way open for a few feet.

A jet of vapour started from the trunk, the wheels of the machine were put in motion, Behemoth and the train advanced together.

None of my companions will contradict me when I assert that there was at first a lively movement of surprise among the foremost animals. A wider passage opened, and the road appeared free enough to allow the train to proceed at a pace equal to a horse's trot.

But at the same moment all the "proboscidian herd," to use an expression of the captain, moved too, both in front and rear. The first took the lead of the procession, the rest followed the train. All seemed quite determined not to abandon it.

At the same time, as the road was here wider, others

walked at the sides, like horseman accompanying a carriage. Male and female mingled, of all sizes, of all ages, adults of five-and-twenty years, and "grown men" of sixty, old fellows of more than a hundred, and little ones who had not yet left their mother's side, but sucking with their lips and not with their trunks—as is sometimes supposed—got their breakfasts as they trotted along.

The entire troop kept a certain order, not hurrying, but regulating their pace to that of Behemoth.

"If they escort us like this to the lake," said Colonel Munro, "I shall make no objection."

"Yes," replied Kâlagani, "but what will happen when the road narrows?"

In this lay the danger.

No incident occurred during the three hours which were employed in travelling eight out of the ten miles to Lake Puturia. Two or three times only a few elephants stood across the road, as if it was their intention to bar it; but Behemoth pointed his tusks straight at them, sputtered out smoke in their faces, advancing all the time, so that they thought better of it, and started out of his way.

At ten o'clock two miles only lay between us and the lake. There—at least, so we hoped—we should be in comparative safety.

Of course, if no hostile demonstration was made before we reached the lake, Banks intended to leave Puturia on the west without stopping there, so as to quit the region of the Vindhyas the next day. From thence to the station of Jubbulpore was but a few hours' journey.

I may here add that the country was not only very wild, but absolutely a desert. Not a village, not a farm —the insufficiency of pasture accounting for this—not a caravan, or even a solitary traveller. Since our entry into this mountainous part of Bundelkund, we had not met a single human being.

About eleven o'clock the valley through which Steam

House was passing, between two great spurs of the chain, began to narrow.

The danger of our situation, already fraught with so much to cause uneasiness, was now aggravated.

If the elephants had simply gone on in front or followed the train, the difficulty would not have occurred. But those marching alongside could not remain there. We should either crush them against the rocky sides of the road, or tumble them over the precipices which bordered it in some places. Instinctively they tried to get either forward or back, the consequence being that it was no longer possible either to advance or retreat.

" This complicates matters," remarked the colonel.

"Yes," said Banks ; " we are now under the necessity of breaking through the herd."

"Well, break through, dash into them!" exclaimed Captain Hood. " By Jove! Behemoth's iron tusks are worth much more than the ivory tusks of those idiotic brutes!"

The " proboscidians" were now only " idiotic brutes " in the eyes of our lively and changeable captain.

"No doubt," said McNeil, " but we are one against a hundred."

"Forward, whatever happens!" cried Banks, "or the herd will trample us under foot!"

Several puffs of steam now gave notice of more rapid movement on Behemoth's part. His tusks ran into the elephant nearest him.

A cry of pain burst from the animal, which was answered by the furious clamour of the whole herd. A struggle, the issue of which we could not foresee, was imminent.

We had our weapons already in our hands, the rifles loaded with explosive ball, and the revolvers charged. We were thus prepared to repel any aggression.

The first attack was made by a gigantic male, of ferocious aspect, who, planting his hind feet firmly on the ground, turned against Behemoth.

" A 'gunesh!'" cried Kâlagani.

" Pooh! he has only one tusk!" replied Hood, shrugging his shoulders disdainfully.

" He is the more terrible!" answered the native.

Kâlagani had given to this elephant a name which hunters used to designate the males which have only one tusk. These are animals particularly reverenced by the natives, especially when it is the right tusk which is wanting. Such was the case with this one, and, as Kâlagani said, it was, like all its species, uncommonly fierce. This was soon proved.

The gunesh uttered a trumpet-note of defiance, turned back his trunk, which elephants never use for fighting, and rushed against Behemoth.

His tusk struck the iron side with such violence as to pierce through, but meeting with the thick armour of the inner plating, it broke against it.

The whole train felt the shock.

However, it continued to advance and drove back the gunesh, which boldly, but vainly, endeavoured to resist it.

His call had been heard and understood.

The whole mass of animals stopped, presenting an insurmountable obstacle of living flesh.

At the same moment the hinder troops, continuing their march, pressed violently against the verandah. How could we resist such a crushing force?

Those which still remained at the side raised their trunks, and, twining them round the uprights of the carriages, shook them violently.

It would not do to stop, or it would soon be all up with the train, but we had to defend ourselves. No hesitation was possible. Guns and rifles were instantly aimed at our assailants.

" Don't waste a single shot!" cried the captain. " Aim at the root of the trunk, or the hollow below the eye. Those are the vital parts!"

Captain Hood was obeyed. Several reports rang out, followed by yells of pain.

Three or four elephants, hit in a vital spot, had fallen behind us and at the side—a fortunate circumstance, since their corpses did not obstruct our road. Those in front drew to one side, and the train continued its advance.

"Reload and wait!" cried Hood.

If what he ordered us to wait for was the attack of the entire herd, there was no long delay. It was made with such violence that we almost gave ourselves up for lost.

A perfect chorus of hoarse and furious trumpeting suddenly burst forth. One might have supposed them to be an army of those fighting elephants, which, when possessed by the excitement called "must," are treated by the natives so as to increase their rage.

Nothing can be more terrible, and the boldest "elephantador" trained in Guicowar for the express purpose of fighting these formidable animals, would certainly have quailed before the assailants of Steam House.

"Forward!" cried Banks.

"Fire!" shouted Hood.

And with the snorts and shrieks of the engine were mingled the crack of our rifles. It was next to impossible to aim carefully, as the captain had advised, in such confusion. Every ball found a mark in the mass of flesh, but few hit a mortal part. The wounded animals, therefore, redoubled their fury, and to our shots they answered with blows of their tusks, which seriously damaged the walls.

To the reports of the guns, discharged both in front and rear of the train, and the bursting of the explosive balls in the bodies of the animals, was joined the hissing and whistling of the steam. Pressure rapidly increased. Behemoth dashed into the bellowing crowd, dividing and repelling it. At the same time, his movable trunk, rising and falling like a formidable club, dealt repeated blows on the quivering bodies which he pierced with his tusks. Thus we advanced along the narrow road.

Sometimes the wheels seemed about to stick fast, but on we struggled, till we were within a short distance of the lake.

"Hurrah!" shouted Captain Hood, like a soldier who is about to dash into the thick of the fight.

"Hurrah! hurrah!" we echoed.

All at once I caught sight of a huge trunk darting across the front verandah. In another minute Colonel Munro would be seized by this living lasso, and be dashed under the monster's feet. Just in time, however, Kâlagani bounded forward and severed the trunk by a vigorous blow from a hatchet.

After this, while all were taking part in the common defence, the Hindoo never lost sight of Sir Edward. In his unfailing devotion and exposure of his own person to shield the colonel, he showed how sincere was his desire to protect him.

Behemoth's power and strength of endurance were now put to the proof. How he worked his way, like a wedge, penetrating through the mass! And as at the same time the hindermost elephants butted at us with their heads the train advanced, not only without stopping, although with many a jolt and shock, but even faster than we could have hoped.

All at once a fresh noise arose amid the general din and clamour.

A party of elephants were crushing the second carriage against the rocks!

"Join us! join us!" shouted Banks to those of our friends who were defending the back of Steam House.

Already Fox, Goûmi, and the sergeant had darted into our house.

"Where is Parazard?" asked Captain Hood.

"He won't leave his kitchen," answered Fox.

"He must come!—haul him along!"

Doubtless our cook considered it a point of honour not to leave the post which had been confided to him. But to attempt to resist Goûmi's powerful arms, when those arms had once grasped him, would have been of as much use as to endeavour to escape from the jaws of a crocodile. Monsieur Parazard was soon deposited in the drawing-room.

"Are you all there?" cried Banks.

"Yes, sahib," returned Goûmi.

"Cut through the connecting bar!"

"What, and leave half of our train behind!" cried Captain Hood.

"It must be done!" answered Banks.

The bar was cut through, the gangway hacked to pieces, and our second carriage was detached.

Not too soon! The carriage was crushed, heaved up, capsized, the elephants ending by pounding it beneath their feet. Nothing but a shapeless ruin was left, obstructing the road.

"Hum!" uttered Hood in a tone which would have made us laugh had the occasion allowed of it, "and those animals wouldn't crush a ladybird!"

If the maddened elephants treated the first carriage as they had treated the last, we now knew the fate which awaited us.

"Pile up the fires, Kâlouth!" called the engineer.

A few more yards—a last effort, and Lake Puturia might be reached.

Storr opened wide the regulator, thus showing Behemoth what was expected of him. He made a regular break through the rampart of elephants, and not contenting himself with merely thrusting them with his tusks, he squirted at them jets of burning steam, as he had done to the pilgrims of the Phalgou, scalded them with boiling water! It was magnificent!

The lake lay before us.

Ten minutes would put us in comparative safety.

The elephants no doubt knew this—which was a proof in favour of the intelligence Captain Hood had argued for. For the last time they bent all their efforts to capsize our train.

Still we used our fire-arms. The balls fell on the animals like hail. Only five or six elephants now barred our passage. Many fell, and the wheels ground over earth red with blood. These last remaining brutes had now to be got out of our way.

"Again! again!" shouted Banks to the driver.

At this Behemoth roared as if his inside was a workshop full of spinning-jennies. Steam rushed through the valves under the pressure of eight atmospheres. To increase this would have burst the boiler, which already vibrated. Happily this was needless.

Behemoth's power was now irresistible. We could actually feel him bounding forward with the throbbing of the piston. The remains of the train followed him, jolting over the legs of the elephants which covered the ground, at the risk of being overset. If such an accident had happened, Steam House and its inhabitants would most certainly have come to an untimely end.

Mercifully this we were saved from; the edge of the lake was safely reached, into it dashed our brave Behemoth, and the train floated on the surface of its tranquil waters!

"Heaven be praised!" ejaculated the colonel.

Two or three elephants, blind with fury, rushed after us into the lake, attempting to pursue on its surface those whom they had vainly endeavoured to annihilate on dry land. But Behemoth's feet did their work well.

The train drew gradually from the shore, and a few well-directed shots soon freed us from the "marine monsters," just as their trunks were getting closer than was pleasant to our back verandah.

"Well, captain," remarked Banks, "what do you think of the gentleness of Indian elephants?"

"Pooh!" said Hood, "they aren't worth being called wild beasts! Just suppose thirty tigers or so in the place of those hundred pachydermata, and I wager my commission that by this time not one of us would be alive to tell the tale!"

CHAPTER X.

LAKE PUTURIA.

LAKE PUTURIA, on which Steam House had found a temporary refuge, is situated twenty-five miles to the east of Dumoh. This town, the chief place in the English province to which it has given its name, is in a fair way of prosperity, and with its 1200 inhabitants, reinforced by a small garrison, commands this dangerous portion of Bundelkund. Beyond its walls, however, especially towards the east, in the uncultivated region of the Vindhyas partly occupied by the lake, its influence can only slightly make itself felt.

But, after all, what could happen to us worse than the adventure with the elephants, from which we had come out safe and sound ?

Our situation was still, however, somewhat critical, since the greater part of our stores had disappeared with " No. 2." It was hopeless even to think of patching up our ill-fated carriage. Turned over and crushed among the rocks, we knew that the mass of elephants must have passed over its remains, and that only shapeless *débris* could be left.

And yet, besides being the lodging of our attendants, that house contained not only the kitchen and pantry, but our store of provisions and ammunition. Of the latter we now had but a dozen cartridges ; it was not probable, however, that we should wish to use fire-arms before our arrival at Jubbulpore. As to food, that was another question, and one more difficult to answer.

We had indeed nothing to eat of any description.

Even supposing that we reached the town, forty-three

miles distant, by the next evening, we must resign ourselves to passing four-and-twenty hours without food.

There was no help for it !

Under these circumstances the most melancholy
among us was naturally Monsieur Parazard. The loss
of his pantry, the destruction of his apparatus, the
scattering of his stores, had pierced him to the heart.
He could not conceal his despair, and, forgetful of the
dangers through which we had been so miraculously
preserved, regarded the disaster as an entirely personal
misfortune. Whilst we were all assembled in the saloon,
discussing what was best to be done, Monsieur Parazard,
with a most solemn face, appeared at the door, and
begged to "make a communication of the utmost
importance."

"Speak, Monsieur Parazard," replied Colonel Munro,
signing him to enter.

"Gentlemen," gravely said our dismal cook, "you
cannot but know that all the stores contained in the
second carriage of Steam House have been destroyed in
the late catastrophe ! Had a few provisions remained,
I should have had some difficulty in preparing you even
the most modest repast without a kitchen."

"We know it, Monsieur Parazard," answered the
colonel. "It is to be regretted, but if we are compelled
to fast, we must fast, and make the best of it."

"It is the more to be regretted indeed, gentlemen,"
resumed our cook, "when we are actually within sight
of the herd of elephants which assailed us, of which more
than one fell under your murderous fire—"

"That's a fine sentence, Monsieur Parazard," interrupted Captain Hood. "With a few lessons you would
soon learn to express yourself with as much elegance as
our friend Mathias van Guitt."

At this compliment Monsieur Parazard bowed, taking
it all seriously, then with a sigh continued,—

"I say, then, gentlemen, that a unique occasion for
distinguishing myself in my business has offered itself,
The flesh of the elephant, as may be supposed, is not

all good, most of the parts being unquestionably hard and tough ; but it appears that the Author of all Things has placed in the huge mass of flesh two choice morsels, worthy to be served at the table of the Viceroy of India. I mean the tongue of the animal, which is extraordinarily savoury when it is prepared by a recipe which is exclusively my own, and also the feet of the pachyderm—"

"Pachyderm ?—very good, although proboscidian may be more elegant," put in Hood, with an approving gesture.

"With the feet," resumed Parazard, "may be made one of the best soups known in the culinary art, of which I am the representative in Steam House."

"You make our mouths water, Monsieur Parazard," answered Banks. "Unfortunately on one account, and fortunately on another, the elephants have not followed us into the lake, and I fear much that we must renounce, for some time at least, any idea of foot soup or a tongue *ragôut* made from this savoury but formidable animal."

"Would it not be possible," said the cook, "to return to land and procure—?"

"Out of the question, Monsieur Parazard. However dainty and perfect your preparations would be, it would not do to run such a risk."

"Well, gentlemen," returned our cook, "pray accept my expression of the great regret I feel on the subject of this deplorable adventure."

"Your regrets are well expressed, Monsieur Parazard," replied Colonel Munro, "and we give you credit for them. As to dinner and breakfast, don't think about such a thing until we reach Jubbulpore."

"I must then withdraw," said Parazard, bowing without losing any of the gravity which was habitual to him.

We could have laughed heartily at our cook's speeches and appearance had we not have been so occupied with other matters.

In fact, another complication had arisen. Banks informed us that the thing most to be regretted was not the want of provisions, not the want of ammunition, but the lack of fuel. There was nothing wonderful in this, since for forty-eight hours it had not been possible to renew the supply of wood necessary for the feeding of the machine. The last of our store was thrown into the furnaces as we reached the lake. It would have been impossible to go on for another hour, so if we had not found a refuge then, the first carriage of Steam House would have shared the fate of the second.

"Now," added Banks, "we have nothing more to burn, pressure is becoming lower, it has already fallen to two atmospheres, and there is no means of raising it."

"Is our situation really as serious as you seem to think, Banks?" asked the colonel.

"If we only wanted to get back to the shore from which we are now but a little distant, that would be practicable," said Banks. "A quarter of an hour would do it. But to return to a spot where doubtless the elephants are still collected would be highly imprudent. No, we must, on the contrary, cross this lake, and seek a landing-place on its southern shore."

"How wide may it be at this part?" asked Colonel Munro.

"Kâlagani reckons it to be about seven or eight miles. Now, under present circumstances, it would take several hours to cross, and, as I say, in forty minutes the engine will cease working."

"Well," answered Sir Edward, "to begin with, we must pass the night quietly on the lake. We are safe here. To-morrow we shall see what is to be done."

This was decidedly the best thing to be done. We were all in great need of rest.

At our last halting-place in the middle of the circle of elephants, no one in Steam House had been able to sleep. But if that was a "white night," as we say in French, meaning sleepless night, this one was black, and much blacker than we liked.

In fact, towards seven o'clock, a slight mist began to rise over the surface of the lake. There had been a great deal of fog the preceding night in the higher regions of the atmosphere, but, owing to the difference of locality and evaporation of the water, it was here low. After a hot day there was confusion between the higher and lower layers of the air, and the lake soon began to disappear in a fog, slight at first, but every moment increasing in density.

This, as Banks said, was a complication which we had to take into consideration.

As we had foreseen, about half-past seven the panting of Behemoth grew fainter, the throbbing of the piston became weaker, his feet at last ceased to beat the water, and the mighty beast and our single house floated peacefully on the bosom of the lake. We no longer moved ; there was no fuel, and no means of procuring any !

Under the circumstances, it was difficult to make out our situation exactly. During the short time the machine was working, we steered towards the south-eastern shore, there to seek a landing-place.

Puturia being in form a long oval, it was possible that Steam House was not so very far from one or other of its banks.

It is needless to say that the trumpetings of the elephants, which we had heard for quite an hour after leaving the shore, had now died away in the distance.

Whilst talking of the different eventualities which might occur in this new situation, Banks summoded Kâlagani to share in our consultation.

The native soon appeared, and was invite to give his opinion.

We were all assembled in the dining-room, which had a skylight, but no side windows. The light from the lamps could not, therefore, be seen outside.

This was a wise precaution, it being just as well that the situation of Steam House should not be known by any prowlers who might happen to be on the shore.

In answering the questions put to him, Kâlagani—at least, so it appeared to me—hesitated somewhat. We wished to know the position which the train now occupied, and that, I confess, was rather embarrassing to answer ; perhaps a slight breeze from the north-west had had an effect upon Steam House, or perhaps a current was unsensibly drifting us to the lower point of the lake.

" Look here, Kâlagani," said Banks, " do you know the exact extent of the Puturia ? "

" Doubtless, sahib," replied the man, " but in such a fog it is difficult—"

" Can you make a rough guess at the distance which we now are from the nearest bank ? "

" Yes," answered the native, after some thought. " The distance cannot be more than a mile and a half."

" To the east ? " asked Banks.

" To the east."

" So, then, if we land there, we shall be nearer Jubbulpore than Dumoh ? "

" Certainly."

" At Jubbulpore, then, we must refit," said Banks. " But now who knows when or how we can reach the shore ? It may be a day or a couple of days before we can do so, and our provisions are exhausted ! "

" But," said Kâlagani, " could we not try, or at any rate one of us try, to land this very night ? "

" How ? "

" By swimming to shore."

" A mile and a half in such a dense fog ? " returned Banks. " A man would risk his life—"

" That is no reason for not making the attempt," replied Kâlagani.

I cannot tell why, but again it appeared to me that the man's voice had not its accustomed frankness.

" Would you attempt this swim ? " asked Colonel Munro, fixing his steady gaze on the countenance of the native.

" Yes, colonel, and I have every reason to believe I should succeed."

"Well, my man," resumed Banks, "in doing this you would render us a great service! Once on shore you will easily reach Jubbulpore, and from that place send us the help we need."

"I am ready to start at once!" was Kâlagani's quiet response.

I expected Colonel Munro to thank our guide for having consented to perform such a perilous task; but after giving him another long and attentive look, he summoned Goûmi. The servant appeared.

"Goûmi," said his master, "are you not an excellent swimmer?"

"Yes, sahib."

"A mile and a half on a night like this, through the calm waters of the lake, would not be too much for you?"

"Not one mile or even two."

"Well," resumed the colonel, "here is Kâlagani offering to swim across to the shore nearest to Jubbulpore. Now in the water, as well as on the land, in this part of Bundelkund, two bold and intelligent men, being able to assist each other, have a better chance of succeeding. Will you accompany Kâlagani?"

"Directly, sahib," answered Goûmi.

"I do not need any one," said Kâlagani, "but if Colonel Munro insists, I willingly accept Goûmi as a companion."

"Go then, my men," said Banks, "and be as prudent as you are brave!"

This settled, Colonel Munro called Goûmi aside, and gave him a few brief directions. Five minutes after, the two natives, each with a parcel of clothes on his head, slipped over the side into the water. The fog being now very dense, a few strokes carried them out of sight.

I asked Colonel Munro why he had been so anxious to send a companion with Kâlagani.

"My friends," returned Sir Edward, "that man's replies, although till now I have never suspected his fidelity, did not appear frank to me!"

"The same thing struck me," said I.

" I cannot say I noticed anything of the kind," observed the engineer.

"Listen, Banks," resumed the colonel. "In offering to swim ashore, Kâlagani had some ulterior motive."

"What?"

"I do not know, but though he wished to land, it was not to bring us help from Jubbulpore."

" Hullo!" exclaimed Hood.

Banks knit his brows as he looked at the colonel. Then—

"Munro," he said, "till now that native has been most devoted to us all, and more particularly to you! And now you imagine that Kâlagani would betray us! What possible reason can you have for thinking such a thing?"

"Whilst Kâlagani was speaking," answered Sir Edward, "I noticed that his skin darkened, and when a copper-coloured complexion becomes darker, it means that the man is lying! Scores of times I have, by knowing this, been able to convict of falsehood both Hindoos and Bengalees, and have never been mistaken. I repeat, then, that Kâlagani, notwithstanding all the presumptions in his favour, has not told the truth."

This observation of the colonel's, which I have often since seen verified, was quite correct. When they lie, the natives of India turn a shade darker, just as white people turn red.

This symptom had not escaped the colonel's penetration, and he had therefore acted upon it.

"But what could Kâlagani's plans be?" questioned Banks; "and why should he betray us?"

"That remains to be seen," answered Colonel Munro. "We shall know later, perhaps too late."

"Too late, colonel!" cried the captain. "Why, what do you expect? We aren't going quite to destruction, I should hope!"

"At any rate. Munro," said the engineer, "you did very right in sending Goûmi as well. That fellow would serve us till his last breath. Active, intelligent, as he is, if he suspects any danger, he will know—"

"So much the more," observed the colonel, "that he has been warned beforehand, and mistrusts his companion."

"Good," said Banks. "Now we can wait for day. The mist will doubtless disperse as the sun rises, and then we shall better know where we are."

The fog was dense, but nothing denoted the approach of bad weather. This was fortunate, for though our train could float, it was not built for a sea voyage!

Our attendants took up their abode for the night in the dining-room, we ourselves lying down on the sofas in the saloon, talking little, but listening to every sound from the outside.

About two in the morning a perfect concert of wild beasts suddenly broke the stillness.

This showed the direction of the south-west shore, but it was evidently at some distance, from the sounds, and Banks guessed it to be a good mile from us. A band of wild animals had doubtless come to drink at the extreme point of the lake.

Very soon we became sure that, urged by a slight breeze, our train was drifting in a slow but steady manner towards the shore. In fact, by degrees the sounds not only came more distinctly to our ears, but we could already distinguish the deep roar of the tiger from the hoarse howl of the panther.

"By Jove!" Hood could not refrain from saying, "what a splendid opportunity for potting my fiftieth!"

"Another time for that, captain," observed Banks. "When day breaks, I prefer to think that when we touch the shore that band of wild beasts will have left the place free for us!"

"Would it be at all dangerous," I asked, "to light the electric lamps?"

"I do not think so," replied Banks. "That part of the shore is probably only occupied by those animals who have come to drink. There can be no danger in trying to get a look at them."

By Banks' orders the brilliant light was thrown in a south-westerly direction. But, powerless to pierce the thick mist, it only illuminated a short space before Steam House, and the shore remained totally invisible.

However, the sounds becoming more and more clear showed that the train had not ceased to drift. The wild beasts were evidently very numerous, though there was nothing astonishing in this, since Lake Puturia is the natural watering-place for all the animals in that part of Bundelkund.

"I only hope Goûmi and Kâlagani won't fall into the clutches of those brutes," observed Captain Hood.

"It is not tigers that I dread for Goûmi," responded the colonel.

Colonel Munro's suspicions had evidently increased, and for my part I began to share them. Yet the good offices of Kâlagani since our arrival in the Himalayan regions, his unquestionably useful services, his devotion on both occasions that he had risked his life for Sir Edward and Captain Hood, all told in his favour. But when the mind once allows a doubt to gain an entrance, the value of deeds performed grows less, their character changes, we forget the past and dread the future.

And yet what motive could the man possibly have for betraying us? Had he any reason for personal hatred against the inhabitants of Steam House? Assuredly not. Why, then, should he lead them into an ambush? It was most inexplicable. All felt quite bewildered on the subject and longed impatiently for the *dénouement*.

About four o'clock the roaring of the wild beasts abruptly ceased. What struck us as curious in this was tnat tney did not grow gradually distant and drop off, one aiter another, as each took a last bumper and roared a farewell to his fellows. No, this was instantaneous. It was just as if some chance disturbed them in their carouse and caused their flight. Evidently they returned to their dens and lairs, not like beasts going quietly homeward, but like beasts running away.

Silence succeeded. The cause was not apparent to us now, but nevertheless it increased our anxiety.

As a precautionary measure, Banks ordered the lamps to be extinguished. If the animals had fled on the approach of a band of those highway rovers who frequent Bundelkund and the Vindhyas, it was most necessary carefully to conceal the situation of Steam House.

The stillness was not even broken by the ripple of the water, for the breeze had fallen. Whether or not the train was continuing to drift in a current, it was impossible to know, but with the day we hoped the fog would disperse.

I looked at my watch; it was five o'clock. Without the mist there should have been light enough to allow us to see some miles round. But the veil was not lifted; we were compelled to wait.

Colonel Munro, McNeil, and I in front; Fox, Kâlouth, and Monsieur Parazard at the back; Banks and Storr in the howdah; and Captain Hood perched on the neck of the gigantic animal near the trunk, like a sailor on the topmast of a ship, all watched and waited for the first shout of "Land!"

Towards six o'clock a breeze sprung up, which gradually freshened. The first rays of the sun pierced the fog; it cleared, and the horizon lay before us.

"Land!" shouted Captain Hood.

There to the south-east was the shore. It formed at the extremity of the lake a sort of narrow creek with a well-wooded background. The mist rose and left exposed to view the distant mountains.

The train was now floating not more than 200 yards from the other end of the creek, and it was still drifting on under the influence of the north-west breeze.

Nothing was to be seen on the shore. Not an animal nor a human being. It seemed a perfect desert. We could not even perceive a cottage or farm under the trees. A landing might surely be effected here without danger.

The wind sent us slowly onwards. We neared the shore. At last we touched !

A better place for landing could not have been chosen, for here the bank was low, sandy, and shelving.

But now it was impossible to move another inch. Without steam we could not advance a step on the road which the compass told us must be the way to Jubbulpore.

Without losing a moment, therefore, we all followed Hood, who was, of course, the first to leap on to the beach.

"Fuel, fuel !" cried Banks. "In an hour we shall be under pressure, and then forward ! "

This was easy work. The ground all around was strewn with dead wood, fortunately dry enough to be used at once. We had only to fill the furnaces and load the tender.

All hands were soon hard at it, Kâlouth alone remaining on the engine to receive and stow away what we collected. This was amply sufficient to take us to Jubbulpore, and at that place we could take in a supply of coal. As to food, the want of which speedily made itself felt, why, the hunters belonging to the expedition were not forbidden to shoot any game they might come across ! Monsieur Parazard could borrow Kâlouth's fire, and we must satisfy our hunger as well as we could.

In an hour's time the steam had reached a sufficient pressure. Behemoth began to move, ascended the slope, and set foot on the road.

"Now for Jubbulpore ! " cried Banks.

But before Storr had time to give even a half-turn to the regulator, furious shouts burst from the neighbouring forest. A band of at least 150 natives rushed out, and made directly at Steam House. In a moment the how-dah, the carriage, both front and rear were invaded.

Before we knew where we were, we found ourselves seized, dragged fifty paces from our train, and held so firmly that it was impossible to free ourselves.

Judge of our wrath and fury when we were compelled to behold the scene of destruction and pillage which ensued. The natives, hatchet in hand, fell to the work of devastation and ruin. Of the interior furniture soon nothing was left! Then fire finished what the axe began, and in a few minutes all that could burn in our second carriage was in flames!

"The blackguards! the scoundrels!" yelled Captain Hood, struggling in the grasp of several natives.

All abuse was in vain, for the robbers could not even understand what was said.

As to escaping from those who held us, it was not to be thought of.

The flames died down, leaving only the bare skeleton of our travelling house, which had journeyed half over the peninsula.

The natives next applied themselves to Behemoth, eager to destroy him also!

But here they were impotent. Neither axe nor fire could make the smallest impression on the thick iron skin of the creature, nor on the engine which he bore within. In spite of all their efforts, he remained unhurt, to the triumph of Captain Hood, who uttered shouts of mingled joy and rage.

At this moment a man came forward. Evidently the chief of the band.

The men immediately drew up in order before him.

Another man accompanied him. All was explained, for in him we recognized our guide, Kâlagani.

Of Goûmi there was not a trace. The faithful servant had disappeared, and the traitor only remained. No doubt the devotion of the brave man had cost him his life, and we should never see him again!

Kâlagani advanced straight to Colonel **Munro, and**
quite coolly, without the faintest sign of shame, pointed
him out.

" This one ! " said he.

Instantly Colonel Munro was seized, and dragged
away, soon disappearing in the midst of the band, who
at once set off in a southerly direction, without allowing
us to give him one grasp of the hand or exchange a last
farewell !

Hood, Banks, and the rest of us struggled in **vain** to
free ourselves, and fly to our friend's assistance.

Fifty rough hands threw us to the ground.

Another movement and we would have been strangled.

" Don't resist ! It's useless ! " said Banks.

The engineer was right. We could do absolutely nothing to save the colonel. It was better to reserve all
our energies for another attempt.

When a quarter of an hour had elapsed, the natives
who detained us suddenly let go their hold, and darted
off in the track of the first band. To follow them would
have caused a catastrophe of no advantage to Sir
Edward, and yet we would have done anything to be
with him once more.

" Not another step," said Banks.

We obeyed.

It was very evident that Colonel Munro, and he alone,
was the object of this attack of the natives led by Kâlagani.

What were the intentions of the traitor ? He surely
was not acting on his own account. Who, then, could
he be obeying ? The name of Nana Sahib came with
ominous meaning into my mind !

     *   *   *   *   *   *

Here ends the manuscript written by Maucler. The
young Frenchman did not witness the events which
occurred after this, and hastened the *dénouement* of the
drama, but on their becoming known later, they were put
together in a narrative form, thus completing the account
of this journey across Northern India.

CHAPTER XI.

FACE TO FACE.

THE murderous "Thugs," from whom India appears now to be delivered, have left worthy successors behind them.

These are the "Dacoits," who are really only Thugs, with a difference. These assassins have not the same object in view, and they carry it out in another way, but the result is identical: it is premeditated murder—assassination.

The Thugs devoted their victims to the ferocious Kali, goddess of Death, and effected murder by strangulation. The Dacoits practise poisoning for the purpose of robbery. They are more commonplace criminals than the fanatical Thugs, but quite as formidable.

Certain territories of the peninsula are infested with bands of Dacoits, recruited ever and anon by such evil-doers as manage to slip through the fingers of Anglo-Indian justice. Day and night they haunt the highways of the wilder and more uncultivated regions, the Bundelkund, in particular, affording them favourable localities for their deeds of violence and pillage. At times the bandits unite in numbers to attack a lonely and defenceless village.

The wretched population has no safety but in flight; torture awaits all who remain in the hands of the Dacoits. Their cruelties, according to M. Louis Rousselet, surpass all that imagination can conceive.

Colonel Munro had fallen into the power of a band of Dacoits, conducted by Kâlagani.

Rudely torn from his companions, he found himself

hurried along the road to Jubbulpore, before he had time to collect his thoughts.

The conduct of Kâlagani, from the day he joined our party, had been that of a traitor. He was the emissary of Nana Sahib: the instrument chosen by him to procure his revenge.

It will be recollected that on the 24th of May, at Bhopal, during the festivals of the Moharum, which the Nabob had audaciously attended, he had become aware of Sir Edward Munro's departure on a journey to the northern provinces of India. Kâlagani, one of the followers most absolutely devoted to his cause and to his person, had then instantly quitted Bhopal. His orders were to throw himself on the track of the colonel; to find and to follow him, and at all hazards to obtain confidential employment about the person of the enemy of Nana Sahib.

Without an hour's delay, Kâlagani had pushed northwards. He overtook the Steam House train at Cawnpore, and from that moment never lost sight of it, but failed to find opportunity to do more. Therefore, when Colonel Munro and his party were installed in the sanatarium on the Himalayas, he determined to enter the service of Mathias van Guitt.

Kâlagani foresaw that almost daily intercourse would infallibly take place between the kraal and the sanatarium. He was right, and immediately succeeded, not only in attracting the notice of Colonel Munro, but in securing a claim upon his gratitude.

The most difficult part of his mission was thus accomplished. We know the sequel. The Indian often came to Steam House; he became acquainted with our future plans, he heard what route Banks proposed to take when the journey was resumed. Thenceforth one single idea and design possessed him, that of securing the office of guide to the expedition.

For the attainment of his purpose, Kâlagani left no stone unturned. He risked his own life, and that of others, under what circumstances the reader will not have forgotten, but they demand explanation.

He wished to disarm suspicion by accompanying the expedition at first starting without leaving the service of Van Guitt, hoping that something might afterwards lead to the very post being offered to him which it was his sole object to obtain.

But the union of the two parties could not be effected while the Dutchman had his full complement of draught oxen, or rather buffaloes. Deprived of them, he would be obliged to seek the aid of Behemoth. That the buffaloes might leave the enclosure and wander away during the night, Kâlagani, at the risk of such disaster as actually occurred, withdrew the bolts, and left the gate open. Tigers, panthers, and what not, rushed into the kraal, the buffaloes were killed or dispersed, several natives lost their lives—what matter? the plan had succeeded, and Mathias van Guitt was forced to entreat Colonel Munro to help his menagerie along the road to Bombay.

He did not do this without an attempt to make up his teams, but this was naturally a matter of great difficulty in the desert regions of the Himalaya, and the business being entrusted to Kâlagani had not the slightest chance of success. The result was, that Mathias van Guitt, with his whole menagerie and personal goods, travelled in tow of Behemoth to Etawah Station. There, availing himself of the railway, Kâlagani and the other shikarees became of no further use to him, and were consequently dismissed.

Banks, observing the embarrassment evinced by Kâlagani, and well aware of his intelligence and perfect acquaintance with this part of India, concluded that he would render important service as a guide, and offered him the situation. It was accepted, and from that moment Kâlagani held the fate of the expedition in his hands.

Who could suspect treason in a man always ready to venture his life?

Once only was Kâlagani on the point of betraying himself.

It was when Banks spoke of the death of Nana Sahib. An incredulous gesture escaped him ; he shook his head like one who knows better than to believe what is stated. To us, however, it seemed only natural that he, in common with his race, should regard that fiendish man with superstitious veneration, and believe he bore a charmed life.

Kâlagani may have had our news confirmed, when— certainly not by accident—he met an old comrade in the caravan of the Brinjarees. Whatever he may then have heard, he in no way changed his tactics ; but led us on through the defiles of the Vindhyas, and finally, after the various adventures which have been related, to the banks of Lake Puturia, amid whose waters we were forced to take refuge.

Then, under pretext that he would seek help at Jubbulpore, the traitor proposed to leave us. Dissembler as he was, a peculiar change of countenance aroused Colonel Munro's suspicions, and he ordered Goûmi to accompany him. The two men plunged into the lake, and within the hour reached its south-western bank.

They proceeded together through the darkness of the night, one full of suspicion, the other ignorant that he was suspected. Goûmi, therefore, as faithful to his colonel as McNeil could be, had the advantage.

During three hours they journeyed side by side along the road which leads across the southern slopes of the Vindhyas to the station of Jubbulpore. The fog became less dense, and Goûmi closely surveyed his companion. A strong knife hung at his girdle. Goûmi, rapid in all he did, was prepared to spring on his companion and disarm him on the slightest suspicious movement.

Unfortunately the faithful fellow had no time to act as he intended.

The night was pitchy dark, even a moving figure could not be discerned a few paces distant.

Thus it happened that at a turning in the path, a voice suddenly called, "Kâlagani!"

"Here am I, Nassim," replied the Hindoo.

At the same instant a strange, shrill cry sounded to the left of the way.

This sound was the "kisri" of the fierce tribes of the Gondwana, well known to Goûmi. He was taken by surprise and attempted nothing. The cry was a summons to a whole band, and even had he struck down Kâlagani, of what use would that have been? Escape! —he must escape—he must fly at once, and strive to rejoin his friends, so as to warn them of their danger. Once more by the lake, he would endeavour to swim back to them, and prevent any attempt to reach the shore.

Without an instant's hesitation he moved aside, and, while Kâlagani joined Nassim, who had spoken, sprang into the jungle and disappeared.

Presently Kâlagani turned back with his accomplice, intending to rid himself of the companion thrust upon him by Colonel Munro—but Goûmi was gone!

Nassim was the chief of a band of Dacoits devoted to the cause of Nana Sahib. When he heard of Goûmi, and that he had fled, he dispersed his men on all sides in pursuit. It was important to secure at any price so brave an adherent of Sir Edward Munro. But search was useless. Goûmi made good his escape!

What, after all, had these Dacoits to fear from him? He was thrown on his own resources in a wild and unknown country, already three hours' march from Lake Puturia; make what speed he might, he could not reach it before they did!

Kâlagani took his measures. He conferred for a few moments with the chief of the Dacoits, who appeared to await his orders, and the whole band was speedily in hasty march towards the lake.

Now, by what means had this troop been summoned from the gorges of the Vindhyas? How were they

K

made aware of the approach of Colonel Munro to the
neighbourhood of Puturia ? By Nassim himself, who
was none other than the Indian who followed the
caravan of Brinjarees !

In fact, everything that happened was the result of a
well-laid plan, in which Colonel Munro and his companions merely acted the parts prepared for them. And
thus, at the moment when the train touched the southern
border of the lake, the Dacoits were ready to attack it,
under command of Nassim and Kâlagani.

It was their object to seize Colonel Munro alone.
His companions, abandoned to their fate in this wild
region, their last house destroyed, were powerless. He
only therefore was made prisoner, and hurried away, so
that by seven o'clock in the morning Lake Puturia lay
six miles behind them.

Sir Edward at once concluded that his enemies,
having secured him in this desolate place, would never
let him leave the Vindhya region alive. Yet the brave
man maintained his calm and dignified aspect. He
walked with the utmost coolness in the midst of his
savage captors, ready for anything that might occur,
and by no sign or look showing that he perceived
Kâlagani. Flight was, of course, impossible, for,
although unbound, he was so closely surrounded, that
no gap in the crowd was available. Besides, instant
recapture must have ensued.

All the circumstances of the case passed in review
before the colonel's mind. Was it credible that this
seizure was brought about by Nana Sahib? Impossible !
Was not that terrible man dead ? Yet it might be that
to some devoted follower—perhaps to Balao Rao—he
had bequeathed the fulfilment of his long-cherished
revenge. Thus only could Sir Edward account for his
misfortune.

Then he thought of poor Goûmi. He was not apparently a prisoner of these Dacoits. Could he have
escaped from them? It was possible. Had he not

rather been slain at once? That was much more likely. But, supposing him to be safe and at liberty, might his assistance be reckoned upon? It was hard to say.

If he had pressed forward to demand help at Jubbulpore, he would arrive too late.

If, on the other hand, he had gone to rejoin Banks and the rest at the lake, what could be done, destitute as they were of all stores and supplies? They might endeavour to reach Jubbulpore, but long ere they could do so the unhappy captive would be dragged into the inaccessible retreats of the robbers among the mountains!

The case appeared hopeless, as Colonel Munro carefully and deliberately examined its bearings. He would not despair, neither would he indulge in groundless visions of deliverance.

The Dacoits marched with extreme rapidity. Nassim and Kâlagani seemed anxious to reach, before sunset, an appointed rendezvous, where their prisoner's fate would probably be decided. Colonel Munro was equally anxious to advance and end his suspense.

Once only, for half an hour at midday, Kâlagani called a halt. The Dacoits carried provisions, which were eaten by the margin of a little brook. A morsel of bread and dried meat was given to the colonel, who ate it readily, not wishing to refuse what was necessary to sustain his powers at this dreadful crisis.

By this time they had travelled nearly sixteen miles. When Kâlagani gave orders to resume the march, they still proceeded in the direction of Jubbulpore.

It was not until five o'clock in the afternoon that the Dacoits abandoned the highway, and turned off to the left. Then, indeed, did Sir Edward Munro feel that he was beyond human help. God alone could save him now.

In a short time Kâlagani and his followers were passing through a narrow defile at the extreme limit of the valley of the Nerbudda, and approaching the wildest and most savage part of Bundelkund.

The place is 216 miles from the Pâl of Tandit, at the east end of the Sautpoora Mountains, which may be called the western point of the Vindhyas, on one of the spurs of which stood the ancient fortress of Ripore, now long abandoned, because when the defiles were occupied by the enemy, even in small numbers, it was impossible to obtain supplies.

This fort occupied a commanding position, which formed a kind of natural redan, 500 feet in height, and overhanging a wide gorge amidst adjacent precipices. The only access to it was by a narrow winding path, cut in the solid rock, and extremely difficult even for foot-soldiers.

Dismantled walls, ruined bastions, crowned the summit; a stone parapet guarded the esplanade from the abyss beneath, and part remained of the building which had served as barracks for the little garrison of Ripore.

One alone was left of all the guns which had formerly defended the fort. This was an enormous cannon, pointed from the front of the esplanade. Too heavy for removal, too much impaired to be of any value, it had been left there, a prey to devouring rust. This piece of artillery, in size and length, was a match for the famous bronze cannon of Bhilsa; which was cast in the time of Jehanghir, and is an enormous gun, six yards in length, with a calibre of forty-four. It might also bear comparison with the equally celebrated cannon of Bidjapoor, whose detonation, according to the natives, was enough to overthrow every building in the city.

Such was the hill-fort of Ripore, to which Kâlagani led his prisoner.

It was late when they reached it, after a fatiguing march of more than five-and-twenty miles. In whose presence was Colonel Munro about to find himself? He was soon to know.

At the further end of the esplanade, a group of natives could be seen within the ruined barracks. They left it, and advanced, while along the opposite parapet the Dacoits ranged themselves in a half-circle, of which Colonel Munro occupied the centre.

He stood, with folded arms, awaiting his fate. Kâlagani, quitting his place in the ranks, advanced a few paces to meet the party.

A native, simply dressed, walked in front. Before him Kâlagani bent respectfully, and kissed his extended hand, receiving a sign of approbation for good service rendered.

His leader then approached the prisoner; deliberately, but with flaming eyes, and in every feature showing symptoms of rage,—intense, although restrained.

He was like a wild beast drawing near his prey. Colonel Munro let him come; he drew not back an inch, but regarded the man as fixedly as he was himself regarded. When but five paces apart,—

"'Tis only Balao Rao," said the colonel, in a tone of profound contempt.

"Look again!" returned the Hindoo.

"Nana Sahib!" cried Colonel Munro; and now indeed he started back. "Nana Sahib alive!"

It was indeed the Nabob himself, the notorious leader of the sepoy revolt, the deadly enemy of Sir Edward Munro.

Who, then, fell at the Pâl of Tandit?

His brother, Balao Rao.

The extraordinary resemblance of these two men, both marked with small-pox, both having lost the same finger of the same hand, had deceived the soldiers of Lucknow and Cawnpore; they had not hesitated to express absolute certainty that that man was the Nabob who in fact was his brother. The mistake was inevitable, and thus Government was informed of the death of Nana Sahib, while he yet lived, and Balao Rao was no more.

He failed not to take advantage of this new aspect of affairs, by which almost absolute security was afforded him. No such indefatigable search would be made for his brother as for himself, because neither had he taken a leading part in the Cawnpore massacres, nor had he the pernicious influence possessed by the Nana over his countrymen.

Nana Sahib therefore resolved to maintain the idea of his death, and renounce for the present his insurrectionary schemes, devoting himself wholly to private revenge.

Never had circumstances in this respect so favoured him. Colonel Munro had left Calcutta on a long journey, by which he meant to reach Bombay.

Believing it possible to decoy him across the Bundelkund into the lonely region of the Vindhyas, Nana Sahib had previously put that mission into the hands of the crafty Kâlagani.

After the affair at the Pâl of Tandit, he himself of course quitted what was no longer a safe retreat, and, plunging into the Nerbudda valleys, concealed himself among the deep gorges of the Vindhyas.

There, with a band of followers devoted to his person, he established himself in the deserted fort of Ripore, where he was soon reinforced by a party of Dacoits, worthy allies of such a chief, and month after month he waited.

Four months he waited, until, having done his part, Kâlagani should inform him of the near approach of his enemy.

One fear possessed Nana Sahib. It was lest news of his death should reach the ears of Kâlagani; for if he had reason to believe it, would he not abandon his treacherous designs?

In order to prevent any such mistake, Nassim had been despatched to meet the Steam House train on the road from Scind, communicate with Kâlagani, and acquaint him with the exact state of the case.

Immediately after doing so in the crowded caravan of the Brinjarees, Nassim hastened back to the fort of

Ripore, and gave him the latest intelligence of the progress of his victim. Kâlagani was bringing him by
short journeys towards the Vindhyas, and he was to be
taken prisoner on the banks of Lake Puturia.

All had succeeded to a wish. This time revenge was
certain.

And now! Now Colonel Munro stood before Nana
Sahib, disarmed, alone, at his mercy.

After the first few words, these two men continued to
gaze in silence one upon another. On a sudden the
image of Lady Munro rose so vividly before his eyes,
that the blood rushed from her husband's heart to his
head. He sprang at the murderer of the prisoners of
Cawnpore! Nana Sahib merely stepped back two paces,
while several men flung themselves upon the colonel,
whom they overpowered, though not without difficulty.

Sir Edward Munro resumed his self-possession, which,
no doubt, the Nabob perceived, for by a sign he made his
men retire.

Once more the foes stood face to face.

At length the Nana spoke.

"Munro," he said, "by your people a hundred and
twenty prisoners were blown from the cannon's mouth
at Peshawur; since then more than twelve hundred
sepoys have perished by that frightful death. Your
people ruthlessly massacred the fugitives of Lahore;
after the siege of Delhi they slaughtered three princes
and twenty-nine members of the royal family; at Lucknow they slew six thousand of our race, and three
thousand after the campaign of the Punjaub. In all,
by cannon, musketry, by the gallows and the sword, a
hundred and twenty thousand sepoys and two hundred
thousand natives have paid with their lives for the rising
in defence of national independence.

"Death! death!" cried the Dacoits and all the followers of Nana Sahib.

He silenced them by a gesture, and waited for Colonel
Munro to speak. The colonel gave no answer.

"As for thee, Munro," resumed the Nabob , "my faithful friend the Rance of Jansi was slain by thy hand. She is not yet avenged."

Still no reply.

"Four months ago," said Nana Sahib, "my brother Balao Rao fell under English balls aimed at me, and my brother is not yet avenged."

"Death! death!"

This time these words were uttered more furiously, and the whole band made a movement as though to fall upon the prisoner.

"Silence!" exclaimed the Nana. "Await the hour of justice!"

All drew back.

"Munro," once more continued the Nabob, "an ancestor of yours, one Hector Munro, first invented the punishment of which fearful use was made during the war of 1857. He gave the first order to tie the living bodies of our people, our parents, our brothers to the cannon's mouth—"

These words excited a fresh outburst of rage among his followers ; once more he calmed them, and said,—

"Munro, as they perished, so shalt thou perish! Behold this gun!" and turning round he pointed to the enormous cannon which occupied the centre of the esplanade.

"It is already loaded. You are about to be bound to its mouth ; and to-morrow morning, when the sun rises, that cannon's roar shall announce throughout the depths of the Vindhyas that the vengeance of Nana Sahib is at last complete!"

Colonel Munro fixed his eyes on the Nabob with a composure which proved that death, even such a death, had no terrors for him.

"It is well," he said. "You do as I should have done had you fallen into my hands." And walking up to the gun, he placed himself before it ; his hands were tied behind his back, and by strong cords he was bound across its deadly mouth.

There, for more than an hour, he was subjected to the base insults of all these savage men.

The brave colonel remained unmoved before their outrages, as before death itself.

Night fell. Nana Sahib, Kâlagani, and Nassim withdrew into the old barracks. Their men, at length weary of tormenting the captive, followed their leaders.

Sir Edward Munro was alone in the presence of Death, and of his God.

CHAPTER XII.

AT THE CANNON'S MOUTH.

THE silence was not long unbroken.

An ample supply of provisions and abundance of "arrack" quickly excited the Dacoits, who ate and drank immoderately, to noisy and vociferous clamour.

By degrees, however, the uproar subsided. Sleep overtook the ruffians, who were wearied by days spent on the watch, before capturing their prisoner.

Was it possible he would be left thus alone until the hour of execution ? Even though secured by triple cords round breast and arms, incapable of the least movement, would not Nana Sahib place a guard over his victim ?

While such thoughts passed through the colonel's mind a Dacoit left the barracks, and came across the esplanade.

This man was appointed to keep watch over the prisoner throughout the night.

He approached the gun, and after ascertaining that Colonel Munro's position remained unaltered, he tried the cords with no gentle hand, muttering,—

"Ten pounds of gunpowder! The old gun has not spoken for a long time. To-morrow she will say something worth hearing."

This remark brought a haughty smile to the lips of the gallant colonel. The most fearful death had no terrors for him.

The native then went round the cannon, caressing it with his hand, and resting his finger for an instant on the touch-hole. There he stood, leaning on the breech of the gun, apparently losing all recollection of the prisoner, who remained like a culprit beneath the gibbet, waiting till the fatal bolt be withdrawn.

Somewhat affected by the powerful spirit he had been drinking, and utterly indifferent to the awful position of the unhappy prisoner, the Hindoo indistinctly hummed the air of an old Hindoostanee song, breaking off and resuming the tune as a man does when, under the influence of liquor, his thoughts gradually escape control.

Presently he stood erect. Again passing his hand all over the gun, he came round it and stopped in front of the colonel, gazing stupidly as he muttered incoherent words. He touched the cords and seemed about to draw them tighter, then, nodding his head as if reassured, sauntered up to the parapet about a dozen paces off.

For ten minutes he remained there, resting his arms on the top, sometimes glancing round, and then again gazing far down into the abyss at the foot of the fortress.

It was plain he was making a last effort against the drowsiness which threatened to overcome him. But at last he yielded, let himself drop to the ground, and there lay stretched, the shadow of the parapet completely hiding him.

The night was intensely dark. Heavy clouds hung low and motionless. The atmosphere was still and oppressive. No sound from the valley reached this height, perfect silence reigned around.

For the honour of brave Colonel Munro we must describe how he spent this terrible night. Not for a moment did he allow his thoughts to dwell on that last moment of his life, now fast approaching, when with rude force his body would be blown to pieces and the atoms scattered far and wide. After all it would be instantaneous, and such a death had no terrors for a nature on which no moral or physical danger ever had effect. A

few hours were still his, they belonged to this life which
for the greater part had been spent so happily. His
whole existence passed before him with wonderful
exactitude. The image of Lady Munro arose. Once
more he saw, he heard that dear one whom still he
mourned as in the first days of his bereavement, no
longer with tears, but with an ever-aching heart! In his
thoughts he returned to the beginning of his acquaintance
with her, then a fair young girl living in the doomed
town of Cawnpore, in the house where first he admired,
knew, and loved her! He lived over again those few
years of happiness, suddenly terminated by that most
frightful catastrophe. He could recall every word, look,
glance of hers, with such distinctness that the reality
itself could hardly have been more real! Midnight
passed without his being aware of it. The present was
forgotten by him. Nothing could disturb him in
his blissful recollections of his adored wife. In three
hours he had gone over every day of the three years they
had spent together. Yes! he was far away in imagination from the plateau and fortress of Ripore, far away
from the mouth of that cannon, which the first rays of
the sun were to fire!

But now came that horrible siege of Cawnpore, the
imprisonment of Lady Munro and her mother in the
Bibi-Ghar, the frightful massacre, and lastly the well, the
tomb of two hundred victims, on which four months ago
he had wept for the last time.

And now that demon, Nana Sahib, was here, only a
few yards from him, behind the walls of the ruined
barrack. The leader of the massacres, the murderer of
Lady Munro, and of so many other unhappy beings! It
was into this assassin's hands he had fallen, he who
had hoped to do justice on the assassin who had hitherto
escaped.

These thoughts roused Sir Edward. With an impulse
of blind anger he made one desperate effort to free himself. The cords stretched, but the tightened knots cut

into his flesh.   He uttered a cry, not of pain, but of impotent rage.   At the sound the native raised his head.
His senses returned, he remembered that he was guard
ing the prisoner.

He got up and staggered to the colonel, laid his hand
on his shoulder to make sure his prisoner was still there,
and in a drowsy tone muttered,—

"To-morrow, at sunrise—Boom !"

Then he returned to the parapet, as if for support, but
no sooner did he touch it than he again lay down and
was soon sound asleep.

After that one vain effort, calm fell upon Colonel
Munro.   The course of his thoughts was changed, though
not directed to the fate which awaited him.   By a
natural association of ideas his mind reverted to his
friends, his companions.   He wondered whether they
also had fallen into the hands of another band of the
Dacoits who swarm all over the Vindhyas, whether a fate
similar to his own might not be reserved for them : the
very idea sent a pang through his heart.   But then he
told himself that such a thing could not be.   If the
Nabob had wished their death, would he not have united
them together in the same punishment, to double his
agony by the sight of his friends' ?   No ! it was on him,
and on him alone—this he strove to believe—that Nana
Sahib wished to wreak his hatred !

Then if Banks, Captain Hood, and Maucler were free,
what were they doing?   Had they taken the road to
Jubbulpore, mounted on Behemoth ?   The Dacoits had
not been able to destroy him, and he could carry them
quickly.   Once there, they could soon get help.   But
what would be the use of it then ?   How could they
find out where the colonel was ?   No one knew of the
fortress of Ripore, the retreat of Nana Sahib.   And besides, why should the name of the Nabob come into
their minds ?   Did they not believe that Nana Sahib
was dead, that he fell in the attack on the Pâl of
Tandit ?   No, they could do nothing for the prisoner !

Neither from Goûmi could help be expected. Kâla-gani had had every reason for getting rid of this faithful servant; and since Goûmi was not there, it was because his death had preceded that of his master !

It was useless to count on even one chance of deliverance. Colonel Munro was not the sort of man who would delude himself with vain hopes. He saw his position in its true light, and he returned to his thoughts of the past, and all its happy days and hours.

How long a time was spent thus he would have found it difficult to determine. The night was still dark. No faint streak of light as yet appeared on the mountain peaks to herald the approach of dawn.

It must have been about four in the morning, when the attention of Colonel Munro was arrested by a most singular phenomenon. Whilst living that past inner existence, he had no eyes for anything near him ; scenes of other days were before him.

Exterior objects, indistinctly seen in the gloom, had no attraction for him, when suddenly his eyes became conscious of something which caused the vision called up by his imagination totally to vanish. In fact, the colonel was no longer alone on the esplanade of Ripore. A wavering light had all at once appeared towards the end of the path, near the postern of the fortress. It went to and fro, now dim, now bright, one moment almost extinguished, the next resuming its brilliancy, as if held in an insecure hand.

In the prisoner's position, every incident had its importance. He watched the light intently. Observing that a smoky vapour rose from it, he concluded it was not enclosed in a lantern.

"One of my companions," thought the colonel. "Goûmi, perhaps ! But no ! He would not be there with a light to betray his presence. Who can it be ? "

The flame slowly advanced. It glided along the wall of the old barrack, so close, indeed, that Sir Edward feared it would be perceived by the natives sleeping within.

No notice was taken. The light passed unobserved. Every now and then, when the hand that bore it waved it wildly aloft, it blazed up afresh, and burned more brightly. By the time it reached the parapet, and moved along the crest, like St. Elmo's Fire in a stormy night, the colonel had begun to distinguish a phantom—no distinct outline, but a vague shadow flitting onwards. The being, whoever it was, was clothed in a long garment, covering both arms and head.

The prisoner did not move. He scarcely dared to breathe. He feared to terrify this apparition, or see the flame disappear in the darkness. He kept as motionless as the weighty piece of metal which held him, as it were, in its enormous jaws.

In the meantime the phantom continued to glide along the parapet. Suppose it stumbled over the body of the sleeping Hindoo! No, that was not likely; for the man lay to the left of the cannon, whilst the apparition advanced from the right, stopping sometimes, but ever gradually drawing nearer.

It at last came so close that Colonel Munro could see it distinctly. What he saw was a being of medium height, entirely covered by a long mantle. One hand alone was visible, bearing a lighted torch.

"It is some madman," thought the colonel, "who is so accustomed to visit the Dacoits' encampment, that they take no notice of him! Why hasn't he a dagger in his hand instead of a torch? Perhaps I should be able—"

It was not a madman, and yet Sir Edward had nearly guessed aright.

This was the madwoman of the Nerbudda valley, the unconscious creature who for the last four months had strayed about the Vindhyas, always respected and hospitably received by the superstitious Ghoonds. Neither Nana Sahib nor any of his companions knew of tne part "Roving Flame" had taken in the attack on the Pâl of Tandit. Many a time had they met her in this mountainous district of Bundelkund, but her presence had never caused them any anxiety. Often had her incessant wanderings led her to the fortress of Ripore, and no one ever dreamt of driving her away. It was only by chance that her nocturnal peregrinations had brought her there that night.

Colonel Munro knew nothing about this madwoman. He had never heard of Roving Flame; and yet as this unknown being approached, and was about to touch and perhaps speak to him, his heart beat with unaccountable violence.

Little by little the madwoman drew near the cannon. Her torch burned dimly; she did not appear to see the prisoner, although she was face to face with him, and her eyes were visible through openings like holes in the hood of a "penitent."

Sir Edward did not stir. Neither by word nor by gesture did he seek to attract the attention of this strange being. At last she turned and flitted round the huge gun, the light she carried casting little wandering shadows over its surface.

Did the poor, bewildered brain know the use of this gun, standing there like a monster; that a man was bound to its mouth, and that, at the first morning beam of light, it would vomit forth a fearful burst of thunder and lightning?

Far from it. Roving Flame was there, as she might be anywhere, quite unconscious. She wandered about to-night as she had done many a time before on the esplanade. Then she would probably leave the spot, glide down the winding path to the valley, and thence stray wherever her fancy took her.

As Colonel Munro could freely turn his head, he followed all her movements. He saw her pass round the gun and direct her steps in the direction of the postern.

Suddenly Roving Flame stopped only a few paces from the sleeping native, and turned. Some invisible power seemed to draw her forward, some unaccountable instinct brought her back to the colonel, and again she stood motionless before him.

Sir Edward's heart beat vehemently, as though it would burst from his bosom.

Roving Flame moved yet nearer. She raised her torch to a level with the prisoner's face, as though the better to see him. Nothing of her own face was visible except her eyes, and they were brilliant with a feverish fire. Colonel Munro gazed intently, as if fascinated.

The left hand of this strange being gradually drew back the folds of its garment until her face was exposed to view, and at the same time she shook the torch until it blazed afresh, and threw a bright light around.

A half-stifled cry broke from the prisoner,—

"Laura! Laura!"

He thought he must be going mad himself.

He closed his eyes for a moment.

Then again he looked at her. It was Lady Munro! It was his wife who stood before him!

"Laura!—you!—is it you?" he stammered.

Lady Munro answered not a word. She did not recognize him. She did not even appear to hear him.

"Laura! Mad!—yes, mad! but living!"

Sir Edward could not have been deceived by a mere resemblance. The image of his wife was too deeply graven on his heart. Sadly changed, but still beautiful, was Lady Munro, and even after nine years of a separation which her husband had deemed eternal, he knew her to be his wife.

This poor lady, after doing all in her power to defend her mother, slain before her eyes, had herself fallen wounded, but not mortally; she was one of the last thrown into the well of Cawnpore on the heap of victims already filling it. When night fell, the instinct of self-preservation caused her to struggle to the margin of the well!—instinct alone, for reason had fled at the horror of these awful scenes. After all she had suffered from the commencement of the siege, in the prison of the Bibi-Ghar, and at the massacre, finally seeing her mother slain had driven away her senses. She was mad, quite mad, but living, just as Munro had said. Crazed, she had dragged herself out of the well, and had wandered away and left the town, as did Nana Sahib and his followers after the bloody execution. Mad, she had escaped in the darkness through the country; avoiding town and inhabited districts, received by the poor ryots, and respected by them as a being deprived of reason, the poor creature had roamed onwards until she reached the Sautpoora Mountains, and then the Vindhyas. Dead to every one for nine years, crazed by the horrors she had witnessed, she wandered incessantly, unable ever to rest!

And this was she!

Colonel Munro called again. No answer.

Oh, what would he not have given for power to fold her in his arms, carry her, fly with her, and commence a new life at her side! With the care and the great love he would lavish on her, reason could surely be won back! But what vain fancies were these? Was he not powerless, bound to this mass of metal, his limbs cut and numb with the tightly-drawn cords, utterly unable to stir, in spite of all his wild longing to tear her away from that accursed spot!

What torture, what agony was that! Far beyond even what Nana Sahib's cruel imagination could have conceived. Ah, if that demon had been there, if he had known that Lady Munro was in his power, what horrible joy he would have felt! With what refinement of cruelty he could have increased the sufferings of his prisoner!

"Laura! Laura!" repeated Sir Edward, raising his voice even at the risk of arousing his guard, sleeping but a few steps distant, or the Dacoits in the old barrack, or Nana Sahib himself.

Neither comprehending him nor seeing who he was, Lady Munro kept her wild eyes fixed on the colonel's face. She understood nothing of the frightful torture inflicted on him, at thus finding his wife again, only when he himself had but an hour to live. She shook her head slightly, as though she had no wish to reply.

A few minutes passed like this; then her hand sunk down, her mantle fell again over her face, and she drew back a step or two.

She was leaving him!

"Laura!" cried once more the agonized husband, as though he were bidding her a last farewell.

But no, it was evidently not yet her intention to leave the esplanade   The situation, already so dreadful, was now to be aggravated in a terrible degree.

Lady Munro stopped.   The cannon had attracted her attention.   Perhaps it awoke in her darkened mind some shadowy recollection of the siege of Cawnpore.   At any rate, she slowly returned.   The hand which held the torch cast the light over every part of the gun.   The smallest spark falling on the touch-hole would take instant effect!

Must he then die by that hand, the one in all the world most dear to him?

The thought was too awful to be endured. Far better were it to perish before the eyes of the Nana and his men.

He must shout and arouse his executioners!

Suddenly from the interior of the cannon he felt a hand grasp his.   Yes, it was true; a friendly hand was busy at the cords.   Then he became aware that a sharp blade was carefully cutting between the knots and his wrists.   By some miracle a liberator was near him, in the very heart of the instrument of death!

One by one the cords were severed.

In a second it was done, he took a step forward! He was free!

All his self-command was required to restrain himself. The least sound would be certain ruin.

From the mouth of the piece issued a hand. Munro grasped it ; with his assistance a man struggled forth, and fell at his feet.

It was Goûmi !

After his escape from Kâlagani, this faithful servant had followed the road to Jubbulpore, instead of returning to the lake towards which Nassim's band was proceeding. On reaching the path to Ripore, he had been obliged to conceal himself a second time on meeting a party of natives. From his hiding-place he overheard them speaking of Colonel Munro, who was to be brought by the Dacoits, headed by Kâlagani, to the fortress, where Nana Sahib had determined his death should take place.

Unhesitatingly, Goûmi crept cautiously up the winding path, and reached the then deserted esplanade. There the heroic idea occurred to him that he would creep into the huge gun, hoping to save his master if it were possible, and if not, to die with him !

"Day is breaking !" whispered Goùmi. "We must fly."

"And Lady Munro ?" murmured the colonel, pointing to the motionless figure, now standing with her hand resting on the breech of the gun.

"In our arms, master !" answered Goûmi, asking no explanation.

It was too late!

As the colonel and Goûmi approached to seize her, the poor lady to escape them leant across the gun. A spark fell from her torch, and a terrific roar, echoing from cliff to cliff of the Vindhyas, filled the valley as with a burst of thunder.

CHAPTER XIII.

BEHEMOTH!

AT this tremendous report, Lady Munro fell fainting into the arms of her husband. Without losing a moment the colonel darted across the esplanade, Goûmi, after giving his quietus to the astounded guard, following.

Scarcely had they passed through the postern before the esplanade was covered with the suddenly awakened men.

A moment's hesitation ensued, which was favourable to the fugitives.

Nana Sahib rarely passed the night in the fortress; and the evening before, after binding Colonel Munro to the cannon's mouth, he had gone to meet some chiefs whom he did not dare to visit in open day. But this was the hour at which he usually returned, and he would not be long in appearing.

Kâlagani, Nassim, Hindoos, and Dacoits, more than a hundred men in all, would instantly have set off in pursuit of the prisoner. One thing alone delayed them. They were perfectly ignorant of what had occurred; and the dead body of the native who had been entrusted with the charge of the colonel completely mystified them.

Their natural thought was that in all probability, by some strange mischance, the gun had gone off before the hour fixed, and that now the body of the prisoner was blown to pieces.

The fury of Kâlagani and the others vented itself in a storm of oaths and abuse. Had Nana Sahib and the rest been after all deprived of the pleasure of witnessing the last moments of Colonel Munro?

The Nabob was at no great distance. He must have heard the report, and be even now returning in all haste to the fortress. What reply could they make when he required at their hands the prisoner whom he had left in their charge?

This hesitation and delay, slight as it was, gave the fugitives time to get some little distance before being perceived.

Sir Edward and Goûmi, full of hope after their miraculous deliverance, rapidly descended the winding path, the strong arms of the colonel scarcely feeling their burden. His faithful servant kept close at his side, ready to defend or assist him.

Five minutes after leaving the postern, they were half-way between the plateau and the valley. But day was breaking, and already a glimmering light penetrated to the bottom of the narrow gorge.

A yell burst from the heights above them.

As he leant over the parapet Kâlagani had caught sight of two fugitives. One of them must be the prisoner of the Nana.

"Munro! There is Munro!" shouted Kâlagani, mad with rage.

And with a bound he was through the postern, and in hot pursuit, followed by all his band.

"We are seen," said the colonel, increasing his speed.

"I will stop the first!" said Goûmi. "They will kill me, but it may give you time to reach the high road."

"They shall either kill us both, or we will escape together!" responded Munro.

The part of the way now reached was less rough, and they could therefore proceed faster. Forty feet farther and they would be in the Ripore road leading to the highway.

But though flight would be easier, so also would be

the pursuit. To seek concealment was useless. Both would have been discovered immediately. The only chance of ultimate escape was to reach the open country.

Colonel Munro's resolve was taken. He would not again fall alive into the hands of Nana Sahib. Rather than leave her, who had just been restored to him, in the power of the Nabob, he would plunge Goûmi's dagger into her heart, and then himself die by the same weapon.

"Courage, master!" said Goûmi, ready, if need were, to shield the colonel with his own body. "In five minutes we shall be on the Jubbulpore road!"

"God grant that we may find help there!" murmured the colonel.

The shouts of the natives were becoming more and more distinct.

On hurried the fugitives; they were at the road; they turned the corner. To their horror there, close to them, were two men, rapidly advancing from the opposite direction.

It was now light enough to distinguish faces clearly, and two names, uttered like a cry of hatred, burst forth at the same moment.

"Munro!"

"Nana Sahib!"

On hearing the report of the cannon, the Nabob had hastened with all speed towards the fortress. He could not understand why his orders should have been executed before the hour he had named.

A Hindoo accompanied him; but before this man had time to make even a sign, he fell at Goûmi's feet, stabbed with the same knife which had severed the colonel's bonds.

"Help! here!" cried the Nana to the men who were dashing down the path.

"Yes, here!" returned Goûmi; and like a lightning flash he was upon the Nabob.

His intention was—if he failed in killing him at the first blow—at least to struggle with him, so as to give Colonel Munro time to reach the high road; but the knife was struck from his grasp, and fell to the ground.

Furious at being disarmed, Goûmi seized his adversary round the body, and lifting him in his powerful arms, actually carried him off, determining to spring with him over the nearest precipice into the abyss beneath.

In the meanwhile Kâlagani and his companions were rapidly approaching; in another minute they would be upon them, and then what hope of escape could there be?

"Another effort!" repeated Goûmi. "I can keep them at bay for a few minutes by using their Nabob as a shield! Fly, master fly without me!"

The pursuers were close behind. In a half-strangled voice the Nabob called on Kâlagani. Suddenly, not twenty paces from them, other cries rose.

"Munro! Munro!"

There on the Ripore road was Banks, with him Captain Hood, Maucler, Sergeant McNeil, Fox, Parazard, and a little way behind them, on the high road, vomiting forth torrents of steam, Behemoth, in charge of Storr and Kâlouth.

After the destruction of the last car composing Steam House, the engineer and his companions had no alternative but to use as a vehicle the elephant, which the Dacoits had been unable to destroy. Perched on Behemoth, they soon left Lake Puturia, and advanced along the Jubbulpore road. But just as they were passing the turning which led to the fortress, the tremendous report bursting over their heads caused them to halt.

Some presentiment, instinct, call it what you will, made them spring to the ground, and hurry at full speed up the steep road. What they hoped or expected they could not have told.

A sudden turn brought them all at once in full view of the colonel, whose first cry was.—

" Save Lady Munro ! "

" And keep fast hold of the true Nana Sahib ! " gasped Goûmi, who with a last furious effort had thrown the half-suffocated man to the ground.

Captain Hood, McNeil, and Fox quickly seized and made him prisoner, and without asking any other explanation the whole party hastened back to Behemoth.

By order of the colonel, who wished to give him up to English justice, Nana Sahib was bound to the elephant's neck.   Lady Munro was placed in the howdah, her husband by her side ; she was gradually recovering from her faint, and he anxiously watched for the least gleam of reason.

All were soon on the elephant's back.

" At full speed ! " cried Banks.

It was time.   Already the foremost natives were but a hundred yards distant.   All would be well if Behemoth could only reach before them the advanced post of the military cantonment of Jubbulpore, commanding the last defile of the Vindhyas.

The engine was abundantly supplied with water and fuel, everything necessary to maintain pressure, and keep up the utmost speed.   But the road being full of sudden turns and angles, careful steering was necessary ; it was not safe to rush blindly on.

The natives gained visibly, and their shouts redoubled.

" We shall have to defend ourselves," said McNeil.

" And we will defend ourselves ! " returned Captain Hood, with determination.

A dozen cartridges were all they had !   Not a single shot must miss, for their pursuers were armed, and everything depended on their being kept at a distance.

Hood and Fox, rifle in hand, posted themselves in the rear, at the back of the howdah.   Goûmi was forward, but still able to take good aim ; McNeil was stationed near Nana Sahib, revolver in one hand, and dagger in the other, ready to stab him if the Hindoos seemed likely to overpower them.   Kâlouth and Parazard supplied the furnaces. Banks and Storr drove the engine.

Already the pursuit had lasted ten minutes. Two hundred paces at most divided the parties. Though the natives went faster, the elephant could of course keep up his speed longer. The only tactics it was possible to employ were to keep the enemy from getting ahead.

At that moment a dozen shots rang out from the pursuers. The balls whistled harmlessly over Behemoth, except one which struck the end of his trunk.

" Don't fire yet ! We mustn't fire till we are certain of hitting !" cried Captain Hood. "Save your fire ! they are too far off yet !"

Banks, now seeing a straight line of road before him, opened wide the regulator ; and Behemoth, dashing forward, left the enemy several hundred yards behind.

" Hurrah ! hurrah for old Behemoth !" shouted the captain, wild with excitement. " Ha, ha ! those scoundrels can't catch him !"

But at the end of this straight bit of road lay a steep and winding pass or defile, the last on this south side of the Vindhyas, which must necessarily delay the progress of Banks and his companions. Kâlagani and his party, knowing this, redoubled their efforts.

On went Behemoth, and now he was in the narrow road with a precipitous cliff on either side.

Speed was slackened, and Banks had to steer with the greatest care. Of course the natives soon regained all the ground they had lost. Though they had no hope of saving Nana Sahib, who was at the mercy of a dagger-thrust, at least they could avenge his death !

Another discharge was fired, but without touching any one on Behemoth's back.

" This is getting serious !" said the captain, levelling his gun. " Attention !"

He and Goûmi fired simultaneously. Two of the foremost natives were struck full in the chest and fell.

" Two less ! " said Goûmi, reloading his weapon.

" Two out of a hundred ! " returned Hood. " That is not nearly enough ! We must make them pay more dearly than that !

And three more natives fell dead.

It was impossible to go fast along this winding defile ; and besides, as it narrowed, the way became steeper. However, another half-mile and the last slope of the Vindhyas would be crossed, and Behemoth would find himself not a hundred yards from an outpost almost in sight of Jubbulpore.

These natives were not the sort of men to be terrified at the fire directed against them. They counted their lives as nothing when the duty of saving or avenging Nana Sahib was in question. Ten—twenty of them might fall ; but eighty would still remain to rush on Behemoth, the moving citadel, and attack with mur-derous intent the little party it contained.

Kâlagani was well aware of the fact that Captain Hood and his friends had but a few cartridges left, and that consequently their guns would soon be but useless weapons in their hands. Half of their ammunition was indeed already gone.

However, four more shots were fired, and four more Hindoos fell. Hood and Fox had now but a bullet a piece.

At that moment Kâlagani, who had till now been very cautious, sprang forward, nearer than was pru-dent.

" Ha ! that's you, is it ? I'll have you now ! " remarked the captain, taking aim with the greatest coolness.

The shot struck the traitor in the very middle of the forehead. His hands clutched wildly at the air ; he made one bound, and fell dead on the spot !

Suddenly the end of the pass appeared before them. Behemoth made one last effort.

Once more Fox's rifle rang out, and one more native sank to the ground !

The natives perceiving immediately that the firing had ceased, pressed forward to the assault.

"Jump off!" cried Banks.

Under the circumstances it was indeed best to abandon Behemoth, and hasten on foot to the outpost.

Colonel Munro, his wife in his arms, stepped down. Hood, Maucler, the sergeant, and the rest speedily leapt off. Banks alone remained in the howdah!

"And that villain!" cried Captain Hood, pointing to Nana Sahib, who was still bound to the elephant's neck.

"Leave him to me, captain!" returned Banks, in a significant tone.

Then, giving a last turn to the regulator, he also descended.

All hurried as fast as they could along the road, daggers in their hands, prepared to sell their lives dearly.

Behemoth, left to himself, continued to move, but having no one to guide him soon ran against the cliff, and there abruptly stopped, entirely barring the road.

On came the natives; with a rush they were upon him, eager to liberate the Nana.

Suddenly a tremendous roar, like a most frightful crash of thunder, rent the air.

Before leaving the howdah, Banks had heavily charged the valves of the engine. The vapour reached extreme tension, and when Behemoth ran against the cliff, finding no way of escape through the cylinders, it burst the boiler, the fragments flying far and wide.

"Poor Behemoth!" cried Captain Hood. "He has died to save us!"

CHAPTER XIV.

CAPTAIN HOOD'S FIFTIETH TIGER.

COLONEL MUNRO and his party had now nothing further to fear either from the Nabob and the natives who followed his fortunes, or from the Dacoits who had so long troubled this part of Bundelkund.

At the sound of the explosion, soldiers issued from the guard-house in imposing numbers. Finding themselves without a leader, the Dacoits no sooner perceived this reinforcement than they instantly took to flight.

Colonel Munro made himself known. In half an hour's time they reached the station, where they were supplied with all they needed, and especially food, of which they were in great want.

Lady Munro was lodged in a comfortable hotel, until it was possible for her to be removed to Bombay. There Sir Edward trusted that his tender care would at last restore life to the soul of her whose body was at present the only living part, and who would be still dead to him unless her reason returned!

None of his friends despaired of the final recovery of Lady Munro. All confidently awaited it as the only thing which could entirely alter the colonel's existence.

It was settled that the next day they should start for Bombay by the first train. This time they would be carried away by a common locomotive, instead of the indefatigable Behemoth, who now, alas! lay in shapeless ruins.

But neither his ardent admirer, Captain Hood, nor Banks, his ingenious inventor, nor indeed any of the members of the expedition could ever forget the "faithful animal," to whom they all agreed in ascribing real life.

Long did the noise of the explosion which annihilated him ring in their ears.

Before leaving Jubbulpore, Banks, Hood, Maucler, Fox, and Goûmi naturally wished to pay a visit to the scene of the catastrophe.

There was nothing to be feared from the band of Dacoits, yet as a precautionary measure, when the engineer and his companions reached the outpost, a detachment of soldiers joined them, and proceeded with them to the entrance of the defile.

On the ground lay five or six mutilated corpses, the bodies of those who had rushed on Behemoth for the purpose of freeing Nana Sahib. Of the remainder of the band there was not a trace. Instead of returning to the ruined fortress, the last faithful followers of the Nana had dispersed through the Nerbudda Valley.

Poor Behemoth had been utterly destroyed by the bursting of his boiler. One of his huge feet was found at a great distance. A part of his trunk, blown against the cliff, stuck fast, and now projected like a gigantic arm. To a great distance the ground was strewn with fragments of iron, screws, bolts, pins, remains of pipes, valves, and cylinders. At the moment of the explosion the tension of the force of steam must indeed have been terrific, perhaps exceeding twenty atmospheres.

And now, of that artificial elephant of which the dwellers in Steam House had been so proud, that colossal animal which had provoked the superstitious admiration of the natives, the mechanical masterpiece of Banks the engineer, the realized dream of the whimsical Rajah of Bhootan, what remained? Only a valueless and unrecognizable skeleton!

"Poor beast!" sighed Captain Hood as he gazed on the body of his beloved Behemoth.

"We can make another—another which shall be even still more powerful!" said Banks.

"No doubt," returned the captain, heaving another deep sigh, "but it won't be him!"

Whilst pursuing their investigations, the engineer and his companions anxiously looked for the remains of Nana Sahib. Even if his face were not recognizable, the finding of a hand which had lost a finger would be sufficient to prove his identity. It would be satisfactory to have this unquestionable proof of the death of the man who could no longer be mistaken for his brother, Balao Rao.

But none of the bloody remains which strewed the ground appeared to belong to him who once was Nana Sahib. Had his followers carried away every trace and vestige of him ? That was more than probable.

The result of this was, that there being no certain proof of the death of Nana Sahib, a legend sprang up amongst the population of Central India. To them their unseen Nabob was still living ; they regarded him as an immortal being.

Banks and his friends were, however, positive that Nana Sahib could not have survived the explosion.

They returned to the town, though not until Captain Hood had picked up a piece of one of Behemoth's tusks, which he ever afterwards treasured as a remembrance.

The next day, the 4th of October, all left Jubbulpore by train. Four-and-twenty hours later they crossed the Western Ghauts, the Andes of Hindostan, which stretch their immense length through dense forests of banyans, sycamores, teaks, mingled with palms, cocoa-trees, arecas, pepper-trees, sandal-wood, and bamboos. In a few hours more the railway deposited them on the island of Bombay, which with the islands of Salsette, Elephanta, and others, forms a magnificent roadstead and port, at the south-eastern extremity of which stands the capital of the presidency.

Colonel Munro did not wish to remain in this great town, swarming with Arabs, Persians, Banyans, Abyssinians, Parsees or Guebres, Scindes, Europeans of every nationality, and also Hindoos.

The physicians whom he consulted on the state of

Lady Munro recommended him to take her to a villa in the neighbourhood, where perfect quie., combined with their great attention and the incessant care of her husband, could not fail to produce a salutary effect.

A month passed. Not one of the colonel's companions, not one of his servants, thought of leaving him ; they wished to be near him on the not far-distant day which they hoped would witness the cure of the poor lady.

This joy came at last. Little by little Lady Munro's senses returned. The mind resumed its natural balance. Of her who had been Roving Flame there remained not a trace, she herself had no recollection of that sad time.

"Laura, Laura!" exclaimed the colonel, as Lady Munro, at last fully recognizing him, was clasped in his arms.

A week after this the inhabitants of Steam House were united once more in the bungalow at Calcutta. Another life was beginning in the beautiful dwelling, very different to that which had formerly been passed within its walls. Banks was entreated to pass his leisure time there, Hood to return whenever he could get leave. As to McNeil and Goûmi, they belonged to the house, and could never be separated from Colonel Munro. About this time Maucler was obliged to leave Calcutta to return to Europe. He took leave at the same time as Hood, whom the devoted Fox was to follow to the military cantonments of Madras.

"Good-bye, captain," said Colonel Munro ; "I am glad to think that you have nothing to regret in your journey across Northern India, except not having shot your fiftieth tiger!"

"But I did shoot him, colonel."

"What! the fiftieth ? When was that ?"

"Why," returned the captain, with a flourish, "forty-nine tigers, and—Kâlagani. Does not that make fifty ?"